A Burglary in Belgravia
by
Lynda Wilcox

D0681189

Chapter 1

Lady Eleanor Bakewell's blonde head bent over the letter again as she read it for the third time. There was no doubt about it. The heavy lavender notepaper with its embossed crest and rounded handwriting proved that the discreet advertisement that she had placed, both in The Times newspaper and The Lady magazine, had borne fruit.

It had taken a lot of heart-searching before she had decided to offer her services as a private enquiry agent. It wasn't so much that she needed the small amount of money she might earn from her endeavours, more an effort to relieve the boredom of post-war life, with its apparently ceaseless round of parties, its vacuous conversations, its sense of futility.

Her recent brush with murder and espionage had reawakened the excitement of those few months in enemy territory before the Armistice was signed. It had been terrifying and, yes, thrilling and given her a sense of purpose in what she thought of as an otherwise empty existence.

She poured more coffee, bit into her toast and read the letter again.

Further to your advertisement in The Times, Lady Barbara Lancashire requests that Miss LEB call on her as a matter of some urgency.

I trust that I can rely on your discretion — as mentioned in the advertisement — and request that you do not discuss this request, or anything that may transpire from calling upon me, with other persons.

Eleanor scowled. Not wanting to put her real name in the advert, she had simply used her initials and a box number supplied by the newspaper. Now she wondered whether she had done the right thing and what Lady Lancashire would make of having the daughter of no less a person than the Duke of Bakewell investigating on her behalf.

It was too late to worry about that now. Ignoring the strictures placed on her in Lady Lancashire's last paragraph, she called her maid.

"Tilly! Will you come in here a minute, please?"

The short, slim figure appeared from the kitchen. A streak of flour marked her forehead and one cheek.

"Yes, my lady?"

"Listen to this, will you? It's from Barbara, Lady Lancashire, in response to that advert I placed in the Times."

She read it out and laid the sheet down next to her plate. "She finishes off with, 'Yours truly'. What do you make of that?"

Tilly shrugged. Well used to being in her mistress's confidence, she knew it was a serious question. "It's hard to say, but I would think that anyone who reckons they need a private enquiry agent wouldn't want the world and his wife getting to hear about it. Everyone who answers the advert is going to insist on that."

"Hmm."

"Do you know the lady"

"Barbara Lancashire? Oh yes, though not intimately. She's a crashing bore who insists on her title, though she only got it by marrying Sir Robert Lancashire, a senior civil servant in the Foreign Office. I've always avoided her like the plague."

"Are you going to avoid that, then?" Tilly pointed at the letter.

"I don't see that I can. As she says it's urgent, I'd better call on her this afternoon. I'll wear the blue foulard dress. It's smart enough for business without making me look like a tradesman, and I'll probably need my fur trimmed wrap." She craned to see out of the window. "Is it snowing again, out there?"

"No, my lady. It looks slushy underfoot, though, so I'll get your boots ready. Are you thinking of walking or taking the car?"

"I hadn't really thought about that. I suppose it will look more impressive if I drive there in the Lagonda."

"Yes, my lady, and a good first impression may be important."

Thus it was that at three-thirty that afternoon, Eleanor drove to Belgravia and rang the doorbell of the stately house in Eaton Square.

To say that Lady Lancashire was surprised to discover the real identity of the person she had addressed as Miss LEB would be an understatement. She flapped about in an agony of social nicety and protocol, unsure how to greet her guest and clearly thinking her unsuited to the delicate task she had in mind.

The servant who had accompanied Eleanor to the elegant drawing room on the first floor was asked to provide tea, then the dithering Lady Lancashire waved her guest to a chair while she remained standing by the fireplace.

Barbara was a matronly woman with a deep bosom, a mass of dark hair worn in an elaborate chignon, and an inflated sense of her own importance. She surveyed Eleanor with a hostile stare.

"Well, really," she remarked, in the tone of a petulant child, "this is most unexpected. This isn't some kind of joke is it? Some jest thought up by you bright young things?"

"Assuredly not, your ladyship."

Eleanor was not unfeeling, but it was only now that she began to realise the slippery nature of the enterprise on which she had embarked. Lady Lancashire would not appreciate the thought of being used only to alleviate Eleanor's boredom. In vain did the younger woman search her wits for a plausible reason for her presence at Eaton Square, or for placing the advertisement in the first place.

Inspiration came in the shape of a large framed photograph on a side table. It had been taken on the occasion of the Lancashires' wedding, and showed the happy couple arm in arm outside a church door. It reminded her of a conversation she'd had with her mother the previous Christmas.

Svetlana, the duchess, a former Russian ballet dancer of some renown, had considered her only daughter to be in need of a husband and, at twenty-four years old, well past marriageable age.

"I feel sure that whatever you may require of a private enquiry agent would involve the disclosure of confidences on your part. So, let me start with one of my own."

Lady Lancashire lifted an eyebrow, but Eleanor was given a few moments grace by the arrival of the tea things. Only when the footman had left and she held a dainty china cup and saucer in her hands, did she continue.

She gave her hostess a brief outline of events on the previous New Year's Eve, concerning the murder of a visiting American millionaire. Events in which Eleanor was deeply involved, though she made no mention of her part in apprehending the two foreign agents who had hoped to rob the American of secret documents.

Her account was punctuated throughout by Lady Lancashire's muttered comments — "Dear me" being the most common — and many tuts and sighs.

"I must also add that my parents are anxious to see me married, and have chosen a young man that I consider entirely unsuitable. However, my father is a reasonable man, and has assured me that if I can support myself through my own efforts for at least six months, then he won't press me further." Eleanor fluttered her eyelashes and, although there was some truth in the statement, hoped that Lady Barbara would swallow the part that was untrue, simply by virtue of mentioning the Duke.

The ruse seemed to work. Lady Lancashire nodded her head a few times and Eleanor pressed home her advantage.

"So, you see, I do have a valid reason for finding myself genteel employment of some kind, and I do have experience of dealing with the police should any crime be involved. And my antecedents are impeccable." She finished with a flourish, and her hostess beamed.

"Oh, yes, well of course."

The woman opposite almost simpered and Eleanor lowered her voice, attempting to put her prospective client at her ease

"Now, why don't you tell me what it is you'd like me to do for you, Lady Lancashire? How may I help you?"

Lady Barbara puckered her brow and spread her hands.

"Oh, dear, this is most uncomfortable, but you see, the other evening I held a small soirée for just a few friends. There were about twenty to thirty people here, all told. All of them are known to me, even the colleagues of my husband, and their wives."

"Go on," Eleanor murmured.

"Well, as I was getting ready for bed, I put my jewellery away in its case, only to discover that my pearls were missing."

"And you think one of your guests might have taken them?"

"Well, at first, I assumed there had been a burglary. My dressing room window had been open when I entered. I'd simply closed it."

"Would it normally be open in this weather and at that time of night?"

"No, you're right, of course, and I noticed the chill in the room as soon as I went in. I suppose I shut it without thinking, as a natural reaction to the cold. Afterwards, once I'd discovered my pearls were gone, I re-opened the window and looked outside, but there was nothing to see – only the wall, and that falls sheer to the ground three storeys below. Nobody could have climbed up that way."

"Perhaps I can have a look myself, later? In the meantime, please continue."

"Well, there's nothing more to tell. My pearls have been stolen and I need to get them back." She twisted her long fingers together in her lap. "It's absolutely vital that I have them returned."

Her agitation increased. Eleanor wondered at the cause of it.

"I take it that you have not informed the police?"

"Certainly not!" Lady Lancashire compressed her fleshy lips into a thin line. Then her expression softened and saddened. "How could I? If one of our guests is responsible..."

She let the thought hang.

"Oh, I quite see your dilemma. What about your staff? Could one of them have stolen your pearls?"

"Impossible. They've been with us for years."

That neither precluded nor exonerated them in Eleanor's book. "But if one of them was in urgent need of money, they might have fallen to temptation, especially as you had a house full of guests at the time. With that amount of people milling around, someone could have slipped away upstairs, probably unseen and certainly unnoticed." She took a sip of tea. "Or do you suspect one of your guests, rather than your staff, of doing that?"

"Well, obviously, I'd never dream of accusing them, and I have no intention of prosecuting. I just need my pearls returned."

Eleanor eyed her hostess keenly. Her agitation was again apparent in the twisting of the fingers.

"I will do what I can. Perhaps you'd be so kind as to describe the necklace to me."

"They are priceless, given to me on the eve of my coming out at the debutante ball in 1898. I wore them, then, for the first time. The necklace is a double string of perfectly matched pearls with a very distinctive clasp. It is in the shape of a rose, that being my maiden name, and the necklace can be worn with the clasp on either shoulder." Her never still hands sketched the form of a rose and flew to her neckline as a means to demonstrate her words. "It is, as you can imagine, unique."

At Eleanor's request, Lady Lancashire showed her upstairs to her dressing room.

"The only access is through the bedroom." Her ladyship opened a door at the top of the stairs on the second landing, and strode on into the room beyond.

Eleanor caught a glimpse of the monstrous double bed with its embroidered satin quilt and drapes in shades of blue and green that dominated the room. The colour scheme was too reminiscent of being underwater for Eleanor to feel comfortable sleeping there and she hurried into the dressing room.

Lady Lancashire's private bower contained a large dressing table with a triptych mirror, two heavy wooden wardrobes, a stool and a small chest of drawers. The room's single window lay along the right-hand wall.

Eleanor took it all in with one sweeping glance, agreed with her hostess that a burglar had not got in through the window, and asked where she kept her jewels.

In answer she was shown a locked jewel case at the bottom of one of the wardrobes. She squatted down to inspect it.

"The lock does not appear to have been forced," she remarked.

Lady Lancashire flushed. "No. I opened it to take out the ruby necklace that I wore that night, then I closed it without locking it. I thought it safe enough in my wardrobe."

Eleanor had been about to ask which of Barbara's so-called friends knew where she kept her jewel case, then changed her mind. The question would probably offend her ladyship, and a cursory search of the dressing room would soon have found it.

They returned to the drawing room and Eleanor took possession of the list of invitees to Lady Lancashire's soirée. She kept her face blank as she scanned the names.

"I will do my best, my lady, though I make you no promises as I'm sure you appreciate what a difficult task you have set me. However, I am at the theatre this evening and will make a start then as I know that at least one person here" — she flicked the list in her hand — "will be at the Viceroy to see Deanna Dacre."

The young actress was currently taking London by storm, in a new play written specially for her. The critics had been full of praise for her performance.

As a result, everyone wanted to see her, including Sir Robert Lancashire and his wife, it seemed.

"And so will we. I'm looking forward to it."

"Then no doubt I shall see you there." Eleanor smiled and held out a hand. "I shall be in touch."

The smile had vanished by the time she reached the street and took her seat at the wheel of the Lagonda. Her very first commission might yet prove an impossible task.

Chapter 2

The foyer of the Viceroy theatre was crammed with the cream of high society when Eleanor arrived and looked around for her friend Lady Ann Carstairs.

She had booked a box in the lower circle for her and Ann and several of their friends. Even the Dowager Duchess of Selsdon had inveigled herself a seat and, if history were anything to go by, would sit quietly nodding at the end of the front row by the time they had reached the interval between the first and second acts.

As Eleanor's gaze passed over the throng she glanced at every neckline on show. She told herself it was a pointless exercise — whoever had stolen Lady Lancashire's pearls would not turn up at the theatre and flaunt them so brazenly — yet somehow she could not help it. The Viceroy glittered with more gems than you could shake a stick at. Diamonds, emeralds, sapphires and rubies were everywhere, as too were pearls, glittering under the light of the chandeliers.

Eleanor's own neck was unadorned and she had begun to feel underdressed for the occasion. She said as much to Ann when they met up at the bottom of the wide staircase, blonde head against the dark one as they touched cheeks.

"Darling, you look wonderful," cried Ann.

"I'm not wearing any jewellery and I feel rather naked as a result."

Ann offered her usual comfort. "I shouldn't worry," she said. "Most of what's on show tonight is paste, anyway."

Thinking it a joke, Eleanor laughed. "Surely not."

"Oh, it is. I'm not kidding. Anyone with any sense has their heirlooms and family treasure locked away at the bank. The rest have them in hock."

"Really?"

Was that where Lady Lancashire's pearls had ended up? At a pawnbroker's?

"Especially now."

"Especially now, what?" Eleanor asked.

"With all these jewel robberies happening, silly?"

Eleanor paused at the top of the stairs to the lower circle and stared at her friend. "What robberies?"

Ann threw her a look of disgust. "Call yourself a detective? Oh, I'll admit that there's been nothing about it in the newspapers. The Daily Banner and the Clarion haven't carried a single report of jewel thefts, so people are obviously keeping quiet about it, but even the Scarsby emeralds are said to have been stolen. Not that Diana Scarsby's admitting it, of course."

Eleanor knew so little about crime and the shady underworld behind it, that she quailed for a moment at the thought of what she had undertaken. What expertise, what knowledge, what right did she have to call herself a private enquiry agent?

Barbara Lancashire had implied that the job Eleanor had advertised was an unsuitable one for a duke's daughter. Now, in the interim between accepting the commission and her arrival at the Viceroy, that same duke's daughter had convinced herself the task was beyond her.

She sighed and brushed her doubts aside, aware that Ann was tugging at her arm.

"Then how —"

Eleanor's question was never answered for at that moment they entered the box and were greeted by the other occupants. A short time later, they all took their seats, the house lights dimmed, and the curtain rose for the start of the play.

Despite not being that interested in straight drama, preferring to watch comedy or go to the ballet, Eleanor found herself enthralled, at least at first.

"She's ever so good, isn't she?" Ann enthused. "And it's the perfect role for her."

"Yes, it is," Eleanor murmured, without taking her opera glasses from her eyes.

The Burning Heart was a powerful melodrama. The actress gave it her all — in three acts, going from the innocence of young love, to harassment and betrayal as a wife and mother, to glorious and vengeful vindication in old age.

The performance was a tour de force by someone so young. Miss Dacre was rumoured to be twenty-six, though many suspected her of being somewhat older.

"Had you heard that she's Sir David Bristol's mistress?" Ann whispered. "He's supposed to have put the money up for the production."

"Yes, so I understand. Judging by the House Full signs every night, he's more than made back his investment."

The millionaire Sir David was renowned for his good looks as much as his money and Eleanor despised the man as much as she despised his politics. She found him cold-hearted and callous. He owned the Daily Banner, a right-wing newspaper much opposed to the newly elected Labour government and its Prime Minister, Ramsay MacDonald.

Presumably it was his money that had attracted the woman on the stage. Eleanor stared at her, surprised to detect a glint of worry and, yes, fear in those expressive eyes, over and above the emotion the role called for.

When the interval came a couple of the men were deputed to fetch a bottle of champagne and six glasses from the bar while the women discussed the play.

"She's so good."

"Isn't she, though?"

"Does anyone know the playwright? I wonder if he wrote it with the divine Deanna in mind."

"Oh, he's had a string of successes."

"So will she. I shouldn't be surprised if she doesn't end up on Broadway after this performance."

"Yes, or even in films."

Eleanor joined in, happy to swap opinions on a subject she knew little about and after Ann's words on the way to the box, wondering how many of her companions' necklaces were fakes.

The men returned, the champagne was opened, and the dowager drank hers straight off.

The play resumed, but of a sudden, it failed to hold Eleanor's interest. Instead she looked about her at the occupants of the boxes, first on the upper and then the lower circles.

She spotted Lady Lancashire sitting alone in the box closest to stage left. There was no sign of her husband, though Eleanor was convinced that earlier in the day Barbara had included him and said, 'we are going to the theatre.'

Eleanor raised her glasses and studied Barbara, whose attention lay fixed on the stage until she suddenly turned her head to look at a point to Eleanor's right. In one hand her ladyship held a pair of opera glasses, while the other lay, fingers splayed, on her right shoulder as if she was clasping something there. In the absence of her pearls, an ugly diamond affair lay around her neck.

The curtain fell for the end of the second act and a sigh went around the auditorium as the house lights went up and the place erupted into thunderous applause.

"Did you hear something just then?" Eleanor leaned towards her friend, raising her voice slightly above the noise.

"When?" Ann shook her head and looked blank.

"Just before the curtain fell?"

"No, I don't think so, though to be honest I was too busy listening to what was going off on the stage. That John Sinclair is a right villain, isn't he?"

Eleanor didn't bother to point out that it was fiction.

"I shan't be a minute."

"Well, don't be long. It isn't so long an interval this time, but if you're going to the bar, you might bring me back a cocktail." Ann's mouth turned down at the corners. "The champagne has all gone."

"Sorry."

Eleanor made her excuses and stepped out of the box into the corridor beyond.

Ann may have been wrapped up in the play, but Eleanor was quite certain she had heard a noise from the box next door. It might only have been the popping of a champagne cork, but it might just as easily been a gunshot.

Thinking that she was about to make a fool of herself, and admitting that it wouldn't be the first time, she tapped discreetly on the door. When no one answered she tapped again and went in.

With a gasp she stepped back. For one wild moment she wanted to tiptoe away and pretend she had never laid eyes on the interior of box number 11, but there was no way to unsee the dead man sprawled over the plush edge of the box. Nor any way to forget the bullet hole in the back of his head.

Chapter 3

One quick glance was enough to show Eleanor that the man had been alone in the box. Alone, that is, apart from his killer.

There was no evidence to suggest he'd shared the box with anyone, no discarded programme, no coat, scarf, or hat left behind in the flurry of departure.

The man's own programme lay on his lap, and a pair of opera glasses were on the floor beside his seat, as though dropped from his dead hand.

Eleanor shuddered and hurried away, along the corridor and down the stairs to the manager's office.

"There's a man dead in Box 11," she told him. "It's murder, so you need to call the police."

"Box 11, madame? But that's Sir David Bristol's box. Is this some sort of joke?"

"Certainly not." Annoyed by the man's dithering, his refusal to take her seriously, she straightened her back and fixed him with an imperious gaze. "I'm Lady Eleanor Bakewell. I'm in the next door box and heard a shot. The man is definitely dead, and this is definitely murder. Now will you please call the police."

"Perhaps I ought to go and see for myself." The manager grimaced and wrung his hands together. "Just to be sure."

Eleanor lost her temper. "Good God, man. He's got a bullet hole in the back of his head. What more do you need to know? Call the police."

With a show of reluctance, the manager picked up the phone and asked for Scotland Yard. Satisfied that the police were on their way, Eleanor went back upstairs to stand guard outside the door of box 11.

"Botheration," she muttered, when she got there. "I should have asked him, or the doorman, if he'd seen anyone leave the building."

She shook her head. The killer was probably still somewhere around. Leaving mid-performance would only have drawn attention to himself, something he'd likely want to avoid at all costs.

Eleanor's lonely vigil didn't last long. She heard the heavy tramp of police boots and the voice of the twittering manager coming up the stairs well before they appeared around the curve of the corridor.

"Well, well. I might have known." The familiar face of Chief Inspector Blount of Scotland Yard scowled down at Eleanor. Behind him came the doctor with his bag and a constable, as well as the Viceroy's manager.

"Good evening, Chief Inspector." Eleanor stood away from the door.

"All right, my lady, you can leave it with us now."

"Thank you. I shall be next door in Box 9 when you want me."

With a sense of relief, Eleanor left the professionals to their work and re-took her seat beside Ann.

"Where have you been?" Her friend hissed. "You've missed the best bit."

Eleanor gave a tight lipped smile, but said nothing. The play was moving towards its climax. She neither saw it nor heard it, and remained lost in her own thoughts.

Was it mere coincidence that Bristol had been killed while watching a play that, if the gossip were to be believed, he had sunk a considerable amount of money into? A play that starred his mistress and was already rumoured to have taken twice as much in box office receipts as the money Sir David had invested.

Eleanor glanced at the stage where Deanna Dacre, unaware of the tragedy that had descended upon her, was in full flow, carrying a rapt audience along with her. At least she was innocent of murder, though someone else concerned with the production might not be.

Eleanor's thoughts went round and round.

At last the house lights went up. The curtain fell and rose again. The cast took their bows and a bouquet of flowers was presented to the leading lady amidst rapturous applause. The curtain was lowered for the final time and the audience started to depart.

Asking Ann if she would stay awhile, Eleanor said goodbye to the other guests and when they had all taken their leave, flopped down again next to Ann and put her head in her hands.

"What on earth is the matter?"

"I've got to tell you, Ann. If I don't tell someone I think I shall explode."

"Well, go on, then, tell me. Are you all right? You're looking dreadfully pale."

Eleanor brushed this aside with a wave of her hand. "You know that I thought I heard a sound from next door at the end of the second act? Well, I went into Box 11 and discovered Sir David Bristol dead in his seat with a bullet wound in the back of his head."

"Wha —"

Eleanor clamped a hand over Ann's scream. "Shh. The police are in there now — it's Chief Inspector Blount again — and they may want to see me before I go home."

"Oh, you poor thing. You do make a habit of finding dead men, don't you?" Ann's dark eyes twinkled with mischief.

There was too much truth in the statement for Eleanor to take offence. "Only in the last month. Come to think of it, I didn't find Henry Eisenbach dead, so you can't hold that against me."

She referred to an American millionaire steel magnate who she'd danced with on the previous New Year's Eve.

"No, darling, he just died in your arms."

A tap on the door put paid to the scathing retort that had risen to Eleanor's lips. Chief Inspector Blount threw the door wide and strode in.

"Sorry to keep you waiting, my lady." He nodded towards the other occupant as he put a name to the familiar face. "Lady Ann, did you go with Lady Eleanor into Sir David's box?"

"No, Chief Inspector, I did not. I've only just been told of the tragedy."

"Then may I ask you to wait outside. I shan't keep Lady Eleanor long."

Ann got to her feet and lifted her coat from the hook behind the door. Eleanor thought she looked disgruntled at being excluded, but she acquiesced to the Chief Inspector's demand readily enough.

"I'll wait for you downstairs in the foyer, Eleanor. It might prevent us being locked in."

She disappeared, closing the door behind her and Eleanor gazed sombrely at Blount.

"There isn't much I can tell you."

Blount ran a hand around his jowls, already dark with stubble. "If I remember rightly, that's exactly what you said about Eisenbach's murder, and you ended up solving that one. Now, come, it's very late and I'm sure you want to get home — I know I do — so what made you enter Sir David's box?"

"I heard the shot, or at least, a loud noise that I took to be a shot and went to investigate."

His eyebrows rose. "Did it not occur to you that someone with a gun might still be in there?"

Eleanor shook her head. That thought had only recently come to mind.

"To be honest, Chief Inspector, I don't think it did. It could as easily have been the sound of a champagne cork, or someone falling heavily on the floor. I did tap on the door before I opened it and went in."

"I see. What time was this?"

"Just before the end of the second act. I can't tell you exactly when that was. Around ten minutes past nine, perhaps?"

Blount nodded. "All right, we can check on that. Did you know who was in there?"

"No, I didn't. I barely knew Sir David, and, as you saw, the dead man's face was hidden from me. It wasn't until I asked the manager to call you, that he revealed the name of the occupant."

"So, what did you do while you were in Box 11?" He jerked his head towards the shared wall.

"Nothing. I...There was nothing I could do."

She told her story quickly and succinctly, telling him everything she'd done until he'd come along the corridor to find her standing by the door.

"Did you see anyone else around?"

Eleanor wrinkled her brow. "No, I'm sure I didn't, although people were beginning to move around as it was the start of the interval. There was no one in the corridor when I left this box, and I didn't hear the sound of footsteps, as if someone was running away. There were a few people about when I left to alert the manager, it was the middle of a short interval, but they were nearer the stairs and the rest rooms. No one between the two boxes."

"And how long between you hearing the shot and entering Sir David's box?"

"No more than a minute or two."

"Very well, your ladyship. Thank you, that will do for now. If you do think of anything else that's pertinent —"

"Then I'll let you know straight away." She rose to her feet and he helped her on with her wrap, the only one left hanging on the pegs. "Thank you, Chief Inspector. I hope you find your murderer. Good night."

True to her word, Ann waited in the foyer. Eleanor found her chatting up the commissionaire, a youngish man who looked very smart, almost military, in his dark green uniform and peaked cap.

"Ah! There you are." Ann smiled archly. "I was beginning to think the police had arrested you. This is Bert, I thought you might want to speak to him."

"Good evening ma'am." Bert raised his cap. "Do you wish me to call a taxi for the two of you?"

"Yes, please." Weariness swept over Eleanor. She felt desperate for sleep. "Did anyone leave the theatre before the end of the play, do you know?"

"No, she keeps them in their seats does Deanna Dacre. No one leaves for ages after the final curtain. Too busy talking about the performance they've just seen. She's marvellous, ain't she? An' she's a real lady with it, always takes the time to speak to me."

"Doesn't she use the stage door?"

"Yeah, she leaves that way, but often comes in by the front, here, and walks down through the auditorium. She says it gets her in the mood."

Ann, much more of a night owl than Eleanor, looked as if she could have chatted until dawn, but at a signal from her friend, simply thanked the doorman for his company.

"If you would call that cab for us now, please, I'm afraid my friend is about dead on her feet." She linked arms with Eleanor who glared at her turn of phrase. "Come on, darling, let's get you home."

A cab soon pulled up and they got in. Eleanor huddled into the fur collar of her coat and tried not to think of murder.

"Are you all right?" asked Ann. "I'll tell the driver to drop you first — your place is closest, and you look all in. I'll pop round tomorrow and you can tell me all about it."

"Thanks, Ann, but I'd really rather forget about it."

"Ha!" Ann laughed and waved a finger at her friend. "But you won't. You're up to your neck in murder again, darling, and if I know you, it won't be long before you've either solved it — or been arrested for it."

Chapter 4

Tilly was waiting up for her mistress when Eleanor returned to her apartment in Bellevue Mansions.

"Did you have a nice time, my lady?" she asked, as Eleanor shed her wrap.

"Yes and no. I watched only part of the play before I walked into another murder."

"Oh, lumme. I take it you'll want a brandy rather than a cup of tea, then, will you?"

Eleanor flopped into her chair by the fire and smiled. "Just a small one, please."

Tilly Walton was more than Eleanor's maid, she was also her friend and closest confidante. The two had been friends since childhood. Tilly was the daughter of the Duke of Bakewell's cook and Eleanor had refused to be separated from her, insisting that the child of her own age have the same lessons as herself, share a nurse, and even sleep in the same room until they were into their teens.

Allowed to roam free on the Bakewells' vast country estate — out in all weathers, watching the lambs being born in Spring, climbing trees, and building dens — the pair had formed a strong bond. When Eleanor learned to shoot and to fish, so did Tilly and when the war came and they were old enough, they had enlisted together — Tilly as a nurse and Eleanor, who had an interest in all things mechanical, as a vehicle mechanic, servicing staff cars and military ambulances.

Now, Tilly was Eleanor's housekeeper, maid, cook, nurse, and protector, all rolled into one.

"Do you want to talk about the murder?"

"No, dear, I don't. Not tonight."

"Well, if it will help to take your mind off things," Tilly said as she poured cognac into a tumbler, "the Duke's been on the phone this evening. He's thinking of opening up Bakewell House. He said he'd call again tomorrow" — she glanced at the clock on the mantelpiece — "that will be later today now, to discuss it with you."

Bakewell House was the family's London residence. Used whenever the family came to the capital and to house refugees during the war, it had been shuttered and closed up since early in 1919. Eleanor's father might be a duke, and a peer of the realm, but at heart he was a countryman and farmer and hated coming to London.

"Did he indeed." Eleanor accepted the glass her maid held out to her. "I wonder what he's proposing. It will take an army of staff to run that place."

Tilly sniffed. "It will at that, but His Grace didn't give his reasons."

Eleanor waved a hand. "Then I'll wait until I hear from him. I'm too tired to think of anything now. I shall finish this" — she raised her tumbler — "then I'm away to my bed. You should go, too. I shan't want you again."

The duke, a considerate man, waited until mid-morning before phoning his daughter. Even so, Eleanor hadn't slept well and, as a consequence, had barely finished her breakfast by the time the call came through.

"Your mother," he said, "has taken it into her head to come to London for the season, and wants me to squire her around the place. Lord knows what's got into the woman. I think it must be her age. Anyway, I'm not paying for a hotel for a month or more when the house is sitting there idle. Will you go and have a look at the place, make sure everything's ship shape? You needn't worry about doing anything yourself, I'll send a crew down in advance to open her up, unless you think it needs major work doing to it."

His voice sounded wistful, as if he'd prefer his house to fall into rack and ruin if it gave him a reason not to travel to London and spend time away from his beloved country estate.

"Yes, all right, Dad, though I may not be able to get there for a day or two. I'm actually fairly busy at the moment."

"That's fine, my dear. No hurry."

She heard him chuckle as he replaced the receiver and smiled to herself before asking Tilly for another pot of coffee and settling down to work.

Barbara Lancashire had invited some forty people to the soirée at which her pearls were stolen. There had been sixteen couples and eight singles, and as Eleanor gazed at the list supplied by her client, she mentally crossed off the majority of people on it.

"Most of these have more than enough jewels already," she muttered. "I can't see them stealing Barbara's pearls."

A title did not guarantee that the holder was honest, upright, and rich, but a more boring, sanctimonious crowd than had been at the Lancashires' Eaton Square home would be hard to imagine.

Thinking herself lucky not to have been among them, but not relishing the prospect of having to interview them either, Eleanor took a pencil and began putting ticks and crosses against the names. "Sir Marston Montgomery? I don't think so. He must be seventy if he's a day. And he's got gout."

"Who has?" Tilly placed a tray with a pot of coffee and a china cup on the table at her mistress's side.

"Sir Marston Montgomery, so he's not going to be climbing walls or even hopping up two flights of stairs. Pfft!

"I'm going through this list that Barbara Lancashire gave me, trying to work out which of them stole her wretched baubles." She twirled the pencil around in her fingers. "I've bitten off more than I can chew here, Tilly old girl."

"Nonsense. You'll work it out. Will you have to go and speak to all those people?" She pointed at the sheet of paper.

"Heavens, I hope not." The idea of making polite, and empty, conversation with Barbara's choice of guests in the vain hope that she might learn something of use, did not bear thinking about. "However, I think I'll pay a call on Penelope Studley-Gore this afternoon. It's a while since I've seen her, and she knows Barbara quite well, as I recall."

"Very well, my lady, and what about the murder at the Viceroy? I've just been reading about that in the morning paper."

"What about it?" Eleanor screwed up her face at the memory. "That has nothing to do with me."

"Uh huh," Tilly said. She knew her mistress far too well to be fooled by Eleanor's casual dismissal. It wouldn't be long before she started asking who, what, why, and when, and sending her maid out to investigate and ask pertinent

— and impertinent — questions of those of Tilly's own class. It had happened before and would happen again before too long. Tilly couldn't wait.

"I trust my name didn't feature in the newspaper?"

"No, my lady, it didn't. I went out early and bought a copy of the Daily Banner as that was the newspaper Sir David owned. There's a small piece about it in the Times, as well, though it's only a couple of sentences reporting that he was shot in his box at the Viceroy."

"It happened too late in the evening to make the earliest editions, no doubt. A blessing in disguise, I suppose, because if the Duke reads my name in his morning paper, I'll never hear the last of it."

Forgetting all about murder, and concentrating instead on the burglary in Belgravia, a few hours later Eleanor drove to Gore House on the other side of Hyde Park.

Lady Penelope Studley-Gore, an attractive woman a few years older than Eleanor, welcomed her warmly as the butler accompanied the guest into the sitting room.

"Lady Eleanor Bakewell, my lady," he announced in a deep voice.

"Eleanor! How lovely to see you. Do come in."

The overfilled room was stuffy and airless. Eleanor loosened her wrap and handed it to the butler.

"Hello, Penny. How are you? I hear you've not been well."

"No indeed," said her hostess. After standing to greet and embrace her guest, she reclined once more upon her chaise longue. "I had a very nasty bout of influenza late last year, and barely made it through Christmas."

"Then I hope you are better now." Eleanor removed her gloves, and put them in her bag, then took a seat opposite her friend.

"Oh much, thank you. Peregrine took me off in the New Year to the South of France to recuperate. We only returned last week."

Eleanor's main purpose in visiting Lady Studley-Gore was to enquire into her friend's health and well-being. She considered it vitally important that her secondary motive remain hidden. Not unnaturally, her client had insisted on her business being confidential between the two of them and, although it placed Eleanor in something of a bind, she had to respect that and find other means than the direct approach to obtain information.

A little general chit-chat, steered in the right direction, might do the trick, and Eleanor was never averse to spending time with those she cherished.

"Whereabouts did you go?" she asked.

"Oh, Menton, of course, though we went to Monte Carlo a couple of times. Perry won a bit of money in the casino there, but then I always said he was a lucky man."

"To have married you, you mean?"

Penelope smiled at the quip. "Oh yes, but let's keep that between ourselves, shall we?"

"Oh, I rather think he knows that already." Sir Peregrine Studley-Gore would be a fool if he didn't realise what a clever and beautiful wife he had and Eleanor, who knew and liked him, did not think him a fool. "Did you do anything exciting in Menton, or was it just for rest and recuperation?"

"It's funny you should say that, given what I've been reading in this morning's paper." Penelope swung her feet to the floor and sat up. She put out a hand towards Eleanor. "You'll never believe this, but we went to a party on Sir David Bristol's yacht. Did you know he'd been murdered?"

Despite the warmth and stuffiness of the room, Eleanor felt a cold hand clutch at her heart. Just by discovering his body she'd already had far too much involvement in Sir David's death for her liking. She wanted nothing more to do with it. Already his murder was the topic of conversation on everyone's lips.

How could she possibly stay out of it?

Chapter 5

"Eleanor! Eleanor, are you all right?"

Penelope's voice cut through the pounding and ringing in Eleanor's ears and she lifted her head and took a deep breath, pushing away thoughts of murder.

"Yes, thank you."

"You looked awfully pale there, for a moment. I thought you were going to faint. I'll ring for some tea."

"Tea would be lovely, but I'm all right, really I am. Tell me more about this party you went to."

Penelope rang for refreshments, then grinned and rubbed her hands together at the prospect of a good gossip. "It was very swish, darling. I wore the Studley-Gore emeralds and a dress designed by Coco Chanel, no less, and I still felt underdressed in comparison to some others."

"Who else was there?"

"Oh, there were loads of people." She tapped a forefinger against her chin. "I'm just trying to think who you would know."

She reeled off a list of names, most of them familiar to Eleanor even if she'd never actually met them — foreign statesmen, film stars, and famous sports players, for the most part — but Penelope surprised her guest by saying, "Oh, that barrister chappie, Sir Petrie Carew, and the Lancashires were on board, too."

"Sir Robert and Lady Barbara?"

"Yes. Thankfully, I managed to avoid them."

"Don't you care for them?"

"Oh, he's all right." Penelope waved a hand as if dismissing the male half of the marriage. "It's Barbara I'm not so fond of. Her husband may be attached to the Foreign Office, but she could bore for England. I have to say, though, that she was strangely quiet that evening, She looked nervous and worried, if you know what I mean."

"Perhaps she suffers from sea-sickness."

"Don't be silly, darling, the boat was moored. We didn't go out for an evening cruise. We stayed strictly landlocked."

"Or she was scared of losing her pearls."

The comment slipped out and Eleanor tried to make light of it when she saw Penelope's puzzled look.

"It was just a joke. I understand she wears them a lot, that's all."

"She *was* wearing pearls that night, come to think of it. A rather nice double string. I thought they might have been her sister's."

"She has a sister?"

This was news to Eleanor and she pricked up her ears, but the arrival of the tea put a brake on the conversation and it wasn't until Penelope had poured and they were alone again, that they resumed their chat.

"I didn't know Lady Barbara had a sister."

"Oh, yes, though Barbara thinks she married beneath her and doesn't have much to do with her."

"Do you know her?"

Penelope shook her head and stirred sugar into her tea. "Only slightly. We were on the same charity committee at one time, until I gave it up. Her name is Marjorie Arbuthnot, she's Barbara's younger sister. Their father made a fortune before the war as a tea importer, or something of that ilk." She gave an apologetic look, "I'm no good at remembering what people do. Do you want an introduction? She's much nicer than Barbara and does a lot of work for the Rehabilitation Society, that charity I mentioned."

"Hmm? Who, or what do they rehabilitate?" Eleanor sipped her tea.

Penelope grimaced. "Well, it started out as an attempt to rehabilitate criminals, showing them the error of their ways by getting them gainful employment. After the war, it turned its attention to ex-servicemen and orphans."

"Orphans? How do you rehabilitate an orphan? Unless they think that adoption is a form of rehabilitation, though it seems an odd idea to me."

"Yes, things got very confused. They seemed to want to be all things to all people, if you understand me, and it was around that time that I cut my ties to them." She rose to her feet and crossed to a bureau underneath the window. "I kept Marjorie's address though, and I'll copy it out for you."

Eleanor took the piece of notepaper that Penelope gave her when she resumed her seat, and slipped it into her bag with a murmur of thanks.

"You're welcome. Do pass on my greetings should you contact her. Now what about you, Eleanor? You look in blooming good health, I'm delighted to say."

"Yes, thank you, I'm fine, though I am looking forward to Spring. I've also been persuaded to take on gainful employment, though I'm not in need of rehabilitation, thank goodness."

"Really? I hope things aren't...difficult for you."

Eleanor hid a smile at her friend's tact. It never ceased to amaze her how the upper classes hated the very mention of money, without in any way being able to do without it.

"No, no. It's more a means to alleviate galloping boredom than galloping debt. Fortunately, my finances are healthy and I just needed an outlet for my energies. Besides, a lot of women are taking on jobs these days. My friend, Lady Ann Carstairs, works as a very successful party organizer. Things aren't as restrictive for women as they used to be before the war."

Penelope flicked at her dark fringe and inspected a perfectly manicured fingernail. "So, what is it you're doing?"

"I've become a Private Enquiry agent."

"Really? That sounds fascinating and it should be something you're good at. You always were...um..."

"Nosy?" Eleanor laughed.

"I was going to say, of an enquiring mind." She grinned. "You like to know things. So, how is it going?"

"Oh, it's early days, yet. I've only just got my first client."

"Oo-oh. Am I allowed to know who it is?"

Eleanor wrinkled her nose. Knowing what gossips people were — especially Penelope — it was a question to which she had given much thought. She had promised her client discretion, and that was obviously called for, but if she was to learn anything helpful, she would have to give out some information, or she would get precisely nowhere. For the moment, though, she remained determined to give nothing away.

"Sorry, Penelope, it's very confidential. I'm sure you understand. After all, in the unlikely event that you had need of my services, you wouldn't want me telling everyone about it, would you."

"No, I suppose not." She looked disappointed and changed the subject.

"You know, Perry has been such a rock for me while I've been ill. I don't know what I would have done without him. What about you? When are you going to find a husband and settle down?"

Eleanor laughed and waved a finger at her friend. "Be careful, darling, you're beginning to sound awfully like my mother."

"Oh, well, we don't want that." Penelope joined in with the laughter. "Seriously, though, is there a man in your life at the moment?"

Not in the way that she meant, and Eleanor shied away from thoughts of a certain Major in Military Intelligence who kept trying to recruit her.

"No, I'm footloose and fancy free, thank heavens. I'm enjoying life as a single girl, despite everyone's attempts to marry me off into a life of domestic boredom and uselessness. I have places to go, and things to do and see before I settle down, as you put it."

Penelope tilted her head and looked sharply at her guest. "You could end up an old maid that way."

"So? I won't be on my own. With so many of our men killed in the war..."

"Exactly! You find yourself a husband, my dear, before it's too late and they're all snapped up."

It wasn't that Eleanor had no time for men, quite the contrary. She just didn't want to be chained to one for the rest of her life — at least not yet. So many of her friends had married and become nothing more than an adjunct to their husband's lives, expected to do little more than play hostess to his friends and look good on his arm.

That would not do for Eleanor.

To her, a marriage was not about being subservient to a man, but a coming together of minds as well as bodies, a sharing of interests as well as a marriage bed.

Besides, a lot of men might want to marry her simply because she was a duke's daughter, with all the prestige and influence that might supposedly bring with it. Suppressing a shiver at the thought, she smiled brightly at Penelope.

"If it makes you happy, then I promise I'll keep looking. Just don't expect it to happen any time soon. Although," she added, struck by a sudden, horrid thought, "Papa is talking about bringing Mother down for the season and opening up Bakewell House again."

"Ah ha! So, there will be parties and balls with lots of eligible young men." Penelope grinned. "I'm looking forward to it already."

"If they are that eligible I shall take them all as lovers, then."

"Eleanor! Really!"

"Oh, I'm only joking. Don't worry, I won't do it simultaneously, darling."

Penelope flapped a hand. "Get away with you, you wicked thing, but that's reminded me. Guess who Sir David Bristol wasn't with on his yacht in Menton."

Eleanor shook her head, baffled. "No idea. Deanna Dacre?"

"Precisely!" Penelope leant forward, the better to pass on what she clearly considered an exciting, and scandalous bit of gossip. "She was in London rehearsing for the opening night of her new play, apparently. Have you seen it? Perry and I went the other evening, and she's divine."

Eleanor picked her words with care, guarding against giving too much away lest Penelope demand chapter and verse of the murder and she'd never get out of there until dinner time.

"Yes, I've seen it."

"Well, anyway, he was flaunting, and flirting with, a Russian countess, Vera Ivanova. It was quite flagrant. She couldn't leave him alone."

"I know the sort. He pours the drinks and she pours herself all over him."

Penelope laughed and clapped her hands. "Exactly. Some wag remarked that he hadn't bothered to dress for the evening, he was simply wearing the countess. It caused quite a stir, I can tell you. More tea?"

"No — I mean yes. Thank you."

The 'no' had been to herself, trying to decline and deny any interest in Bristol's murder. But, while one part of her mind was telling her that it had nothing to do with Eleanor Bakewell, and that Eleanor Bakewell was not, under any circumstances, getting involved, the other part was yelling that Deanna Dacre now had a motive.

Impossible, she thought. The woman was on the stage in full view of a packed theatre all hanging on her every word, expression, posture, and hand movement. There was no way she could simultaneously commit murder.

She passed her cup and saucer over to Penelope. "I wonder if Deanna knew her backer was playing the field."

"Somebody might have told her. There were enough people on the yacht that evening, and that sort of news would travel quickly. Gossip always does."

"Do you think he was serious about the Countess Ivanova?"

"Heavens no, but I bet if she's heard, the Dacre woman is furious."

Chapter 6

After her interview with Lady Penelope, Eleanor decided on a quiet night at home. There was time yet to call on Marjorie Arbuthnot and the others on Lady Barbara's guest list. In the meantime, she would enjoy Tilly's excellent roast chicken, relax, and read her book.

Like all the best laid plans, though, this one took its own divergent path almost as soon as she'd finished her meal.

Tilly had answered the knock on the door and came back with a face like thunder.

"Major Armitage to see you, my lady."

Eleanor struggled to keep her own face grimace free. "Thank you. Tilly, please show him in."

The two women had first met Peter Armitage, who worked for Military Intelligence, during the war. With their respective skills, Eleanor and Tilly had been recruited into his unit for a daring espionage raid across the Channel. More recent contact had come only a month ago when Eleanor, with her maid's assistance, had helped to thwart a couple of spies intending to intercept a secret steel-making formula before it reached the British government.

Eleanor sighed. Whatever he wanted now would not be good news for her peace of mind.

"Good evening, Lady Eleanor. I trust you are well?" The major handed his hat and coat to Tilly.

The maid sniffed, closing the door with a bang as she went out and left her mistress and the major together.

"Fine, thank you, Peter." She indicated a chair by the fire. "May I get you a drink?"

"No, I'm fine, thanks, but don't let me stop you."

"You won't," she said, and crossed to the drinks trolley under the side window. She splashed a little cognac into a tumbler. "To what do I owe the...pleasure?"

"I need your help again, seeing as you are already mixed up in this business."

"Which business, pray?" Her tone was glacial.

She resumed her seat and stared across the space between them. His handsome face appeared haggard, the scar on the left side of his chin showing livid on his clenched jaw. The dark hair that sprang up from his forehead and curled around his ears badly needed a trim.

The man was trouble writ large. Wishing she'd had the sense to send him away, or to tell Tilly that she wasn't at home, she waited, ignoring the thrill of excitement she always felt when he was near.

"Please don't play games with me, Lady Eleanor. There isn't time. We have ten days to prevent a man's death, an incident that could plunge us into war again."

Was the man raving? She had no idea what he was talking about, nor was she happy about him using the word 'we'. Was it a reference to the department in Military Intelligence that he worked for, or something more personal?

"I'm sorry to hear that, Major, but what has it to do with me? I'm not clairvoyant. Explain yourself."

"You know I can't do that."

It took every ounce of Eleanor's self-control and impeccable breeding to stop her from pounding the arm of her chair. "Damn it, Peter. You come here asking my help, then expect me to divine it for myself? I know you work for Military Intelligence, I know you deal in secrets that cannot be shared with outsiders, but if you don't share with me, if you don't trust me, then I'm in no position to help you."

He rubbed the back of his neck and scowled at her. He gave a brief nod, as though he had come to some decision.

"You're right, of course. It's just that it goes against the grain, you see?"

"Perfectly. Now, what is it you'd like me to do?"

Armitage took a deep breath. "We've suspected for a long time that Sir David Bristol was passing on state secrets and information to our enemies. We just don't know how. He occasionally hosted meetings with both German and Russian businessmen at his home in Berkshire."

"Then there's your answer." It was obvious, but Armitage was not a stupid man. There must be more to it than that. "Surely, though, with Bristol's death that problem has been removed?"

"Perhaps. Frankly, whoever killed him did us a favour, in one sense. However, we still don't know who was passing him the information from our side. That's where you come in."

Biting back her first angry retort that if he thought he could make her dance to his own tune then he had better think again, Eleanor gazed into her brandy glass. "I do?" she asked in a quiet voice.

"Yes. I'd be interested to know your thoughts concerning Sir Oswald Brain, Gerald Hope-Weedon, and Sir Robert Lancashire."

Surprised that Armitage had included Lady Barbara's husband on his list, and that Hope-Weedon was a name on the list of attendees for that lady's soirée, the hand in which Eleanor held her glass shook, splashing liquid onto her fingers.

"You know the names?" he asked.

"Yes, of course I do. They are all senior civil servants or government ministers working in the Foreign Office. That doesn't mean to say that I know them well, or even at all. The aristocracy aren't forever in each other's pockets, you know, much as you seem to think they are."

Unperturbed by her frosty reply, he said, "So, what can you tell me about them?"

Eleanor sighed and pursed her lips. "Well...Sir Oswald Brain hasn't got one. A more stupid and incompetent man it would be hard to meet. Comes from a long line of landed gentry and likes to boast that he can trace his family as far back as before Cromwell's time - Thomas Cromwell, that is — so they've had long enough to breed the brain out of the male line, at least.

"I've never met Gerald Hope-Weedon. At least, I don't think so. A self-made man, so I hear.

"As for Sir Robert Lancashire, gossip has it that he was hoping to be the Secretary of State for Foreign Affairs, but MacDonald took on that role as well as Prime Minister. By sheer coincidence, I've just taken on a commission from Sir Robert's wife. She's a bore and so is he, though in a more bumbling sort of way than she is."

She sipped her cognac. "Does that help?" She looked up and caught him laughing.

"You always were a wonderful observer. Your assessment of Sir Oswald is a little unkind ..."

"But accurate."

"Granted." He became suddenly serious. "Our problem is that we suspect one of the three to be responsible for the leak in information. Now, if it is Sir Oswald then, given what you say of him, the leak may be inadvertent. As for the other two..." He shrugged.

"I don't know what you think I can do about it, Major. I can pay courtesy calls upon their wives, I can accost them if I see them at the theatre, or a party, or soirée, but I can hardly come straight out and ask them if they're traitors. Nor do I intend listening at closed doors or entering private studies and reading their correspondence. I've told you before, I won't snoop for you."

When the Armistice had been signed in November 1918, Eleanor had sworn that she would never get involved with espionage again. She might be very attracted to Peter Armitage, his dark, almost saturnine good looks and piercing intelligence assured that, but she cursed his insistence on dragging her into his business.

"I'm hardly asking you to do that," he said, in a placatory tone. "I'd merely like you to keep your ears and eyes open and report anything that you think relevant to me. Would you do that for me, please?"

His soft spoken polite request did not fool her. She could certainly comply with it, none of the three people he'd mentioned were her friends or bosom buddies. She might not feel so sanguine reporting them if they were. Besides, with the exception of the Lancashires, she was unlikely to encounter any of them, and wasn't going to go out of her way to do so.

"Very well. Anyway, what has all this to do with ten days to prevent murder and war?"

"As you were the one to discover Bristol's body, do you intend investigating his death?

"Certainly not. I shall leave that to the police."

"Hmm. A pity."

Eleanor gaped at him. "What on earth do you mean by that, Major?"

In answer he got to his feet and circled the comfortable armchair he'd been sitting on. Brows drawn down, he repeated the exercise before resuming his seat.

"Listen, my lady. In ten days the Prime Minister will have a meeting with a French politician by the name of Gaston Doumergue. Ramsay MacDonald may have the first ever Labour government in Britain, but it's a minority one. A lot of people would like to see the back of it."

"But he's only been in power for a little over a week. Can't they give the man a chance?"

"Ha! You know it doesn't work like that. Power, or the wanting of it, leads to all sorts of machinations."

Eleanor's face twisted in a sour grimace. "Go on. About the meeting with Mr Doumergue."

"It's due to take place at Chequers, though the date is a closely guarded secret, and we've received information that there is to be an assassination attempt."

"Upon whom?"

"Doumergue. We think the idea is to discredit MacDonald, and force another election. Mr Doumergue's party of radical socialists would not be too happy, either. He is expected to become the next President of France."

Eleanor's head was spinning with all these names and allegiances. "Bah! Politics. Damn all politicians to perdition."

"It could lead to war."

"What? Between Britain and France? Nonsense!"

Eleanor tossed her head. Armitage's claim didn't scare her. She was not to be coerced into meddling in matters she considered did not concern her just because the Major was unable to solve his own problems. Was his department so short of staff, or was there no intelligence in the Military Intelligence office?

"Well, we must hope that it won't come to that, but Bristol was involved in the plot. Someone was feeding him information."

"But, surely, that is immaterial now that he's dead. Chief Inspector Blount is a capable man, he'll find your killer for you."

"But Blount cannot mix with the high-and-mighty like you do. They'd close ranks on him and shut up tighter than a clam, yet it's within those ranks that we need to look for both a traitor and a killer. That's where you come in."

"Really, Major! You are impossible. How many times do I have to tell you that I will not get involved? I cannot help you."

He got to his feet. "Very well."

Eleanor rang for her maid who brought Armitage's hat and coat. Happy to be seeing the back of him, Eleanor showed him to the door.

"Good night, your ladyship." He settled the hat on his head. "You'll let me know what you find out, won't you?"

With an unladylike display of temper, Eleanor slammed the door in his face.

Chapter 7

Tilly was waiting for her when Eleanor returned to the drawing room. She stood in front of the kitchen door, arms crossed, and with a furious scowl on her face.

"He's got a nerve," she said.

"Hasn't he just? Did you hear what he wanted?"

Resenting the implication that she had been eavesdropping, Tilly's scowl deepened. "Certainly not." She pointed a thumb over her shoulder. "I was in there ironing, with the door closed."

Eleanor grinned. "That's a shame. I was hoping you could tell me." She took her seat and motioned for Tilly to join her. "I really don't know why he came, or what it is he wants me to do."

"As to why he came, that's obvious."

"Oh?"

"Yes, he's sweet on you, my lady."

"Nonsense, Tilly, old girl. He was telling me about some plot to assassinate a politician and start a war which he thinks I can prevent by solving the murder of Sir David Bristol."

"Humph. Now that is nonsense. I hope you sent him away with a flea in his ear."

"Oh, yes. You heard the front door bang."

Tilly's face lit up with a broad smile. "I should think they heard it in Piccadilly Circus. Well done, my lady."

"Oh, I'm not proud of myself. Peter Armitage has a way of riling me like no other man I know. I wish he would leave me alone."

Yet he wouldn't. Even in bed that evening, searching for sleep, her thoughts were full of him.

She and Tilly had both been a few months short of eighteen when they'd enlisted. The maid had cut Eleanor's long blonde hair and dyed the remaining locks black. When they had volunteered for Military Intelligence, Eleanor, fearing rejection if her true name and status were known, gave her name as Ella Rowsley.

They had been assigned to Major Armitage's small unit and, in 1918, six of them had travelled to France and onwards into the forest of the Ardennes.

A series of dangerous missions followed, including the planting of false information, the rescue of an important prisoner, and acts of sabotage and vandalism. Three months of living on the edge when death may come at every turn and every false step, thrown together and living cheek by jowl, it was no wonder that she and the major had found solace in each other's arms.

With their tasks accomplished, the group had split up. Tilly went north with two of the men, while Eleanor and the major and the other man in the party headed west, moving, always moving, waiting for the signal to pull out and the long trek across to the coast.

There, on the beach at the little fishing village of St Valery sur Somme, on a star-filled night, Eleanor and Armitage had made love again, before the arrival of the boat that would take them to safety. There might have been a third time, except for the sudden storm that blew up. In the cramped cabin, gripped by seasickness, Eleanor wanted only to lie on the narrow bunk and wait for death to claim her.

It hadn't, and once they'd reached London and made their reports, she had slipped away to find Tilly, whose group had also arrived safely a mere twelve hours before them. Then she had gone home, taking her maid with her, telling no one, for no one knew her true identity or where her real home was.

In the safety of Bakewell Park, they had re-built their lives, and moved on. If Peter Armitage thought he could draw her back into his seedy world, he was very wrong. The time she had spent with him had been thrilling, exciting, and terrifying, but it was over. Tomorrow she would forget all about him and concentrate on locating Barbara Lancashire's pearls.

The next morning, Eleanor ordered her car brought around from the garage at the rear of Bellevue Mansions and drove her beloved Lagonda to an address in Maida Vale. She parked in front of a neat Victorian villa and knocked on the door.

Marjorie Arbuthnot bore little or no resemblance to her older sister. Where Barbara was thickset and well-corseted, Marjorie was slim and lithe with masses of chestnut brown hair that appeared to owe nothing to the hairdresser's art. She wore it in a neat plait that stretched past her shoulder blades. It was not a fashionable style, and it marked her out as her own woman.

A pair of fine green eyes surveyed the card that Eleanor had just presented, then looked up and smiled.

"Do come in, your ladyship. I've just brewed a jug of coffee, if you'd like some?"

"That would be very kind, thank you."

Eleanor sat on a roomy sofa and gazed around while her hostess fetched another cup and saucer.

Compared to the overstuffed room at Eaton Square, Marjorie's living space was light and airy. The pastel coloured curtains and furnishings in yellow and pale green gave the room a springlike feel that was enhanced by the bowl of early hyacinths on an occasional table. The air was heady with their scent.

By the time her hostess returned with the coffee, Eleanor knew what she was going to say and, after a few pleasantries, broached the reason for her visit.

"Please forgive me calling on you like this, Mrs Arbuthnot. I appreciate that it is something of an imposition but, in my capacity as a private enquiry agent, I've been retained by Lady Barbara Lancashire to look into a matter of some concern to her."

"Barbara?" Marjorie appeared startled at the name. "I trust she and Robert are well. I can't imagine Barbara letting anything concern her, quite frankly."

Eleanor sipped hot coffee and gazed at Marjorie over the rim of her cup. "Do you not get on with her?"

"Not really. It's merely a matter of sibling rivalry. I take it you know we are sisters?"

"Yes."

"Well, in that case you should know that Barbara thinks I married beneath me, and I think she is a snob. Robert may have a title, but he is only a civil servant in the Foreign Office, and a bumbling one at that. He is quite the most forgetful man I know, always leaving things behind or not locking things away. Anyway, Barbara and I have little to do with each other, which is exactly the way I like it."

Not every pair of sisters liked each other nor every sister and brother. Eleanor thought of her own sibling, Michael, back home in Derbyshire and was suddenly grateful for the good relationship they had. It was a surprise, though, that Marjorie hadn't even asked what problem beset her sister.

"I see, then it seems I may have wasted your time."

"I cannot see that I can help you, my lady. Still, as you are here, I might as well hear what it is you thought I could do. What is it that is bothering Barbara enough that she should need a private detective?"

"It is a delicate matter, Mrs Arbuthnot, and I did assure Lady Lancashire of my discretion..."

"But too much discretion will get you nowhere, eh?" She threw back her head and laughed. "How typical of Barbara to employ someone and then effectively hamstring them. Go on, my lady, out with it. Barbara's secret is safe with me."

Eleanor smiled. There was something very appealing about Marjorie Arbuthnot. There would always be laughter and good humour in this house. There would be time for friends and neighbours, time to talk and be companionable, to share life's trials and tribulations as well as its triumphs. Time, indeed, for people and not possessions.

A bigger contrast to Barbara and her residence was hard to imagine.

"Very well. It has to do with a pearl necklace. Unique and priceless, I understand."

"Poppycock!"

Eleanor nearly dropped her coffee. To be on the safe side — Tilly would grumble if the dress became stained — she put the cup and saucer on the tray and threw Marjorie a questioning glance.

"Oh? How so."

"For a start, it was not unique."

"Then why —"

"I see that I had better tell you the whole story."

Eleanor settled back prepared to listen and was surprised when her hostess got to her feet and with a murmured "excuse me", went out of the room. She heard her footsteps going up the stairs and crossing overhead, but in less than a minute Marjorie returned with a framed photograph in her hand.

She resumed her seat. "My father spent all his life in the tea trade. He had no title, though he rose to be the chairman of the Guild of Tea Importers and Merchants. By his standards, and mine come to that, he grew to be a wealthy man.

"Unfortunately for him, he had no son, but he did have three daughters, Barbara, myself, and Amy. She died young, but not before Father had commissioned three identical pearl necklaces for us. His idea was that he would present them to us and we would wear them at our coming out parties."

She reached for the coffee pot and refilled her cup, then swung the pot in Eleanor's direction.

"No, thank you, I'm fine."

Marjorie put the pot down and passed the photograph to her guest. "Here we are wearing them." She poured cream into her coffee, picked up the cup, and sat back. "It was the first and last time I ever wore them. I appreciate that it makes me sound like a dreadful ingrate, and if the necklaces had all been different from one another, then I would have worn mine gladly, but there was no way I was going to wear it for my coming out do and have everybody thinking that I had borrowed Barbara's pearls. I wore enough of her hand-me-down stuff as it was."

"Have you still got them?"

"No, when Father gave them to me, he said they were mine, unconditionally, so I sold them when Geoffrey and I were married and used the money to buy this house."

That was a pity.

Eleanor clearly remembered the interview with her client regarding the necklace. Lady Lancashire had been quite vehement about it, and her words had been very specific. She hadn't said 'I want it back', but 'I need it back'. Only now did Eleanor come to wonder at the choice of words.

If the need was that great, then it might have been possible to have borrowed Marjorie's. Unless...

"Does Lady Lancashire know that you parted with it?"

"Yes, I rather think she does."

"And the third necklace?"

"Was buried with Amy."

"I see."

Eleanor looked at the photograph closely. It must have been taken shortly after the necklaces were bought. It showed Marjorie, perhaps in her mid-teens, standing between Barbara and a younger girl.

The necklaces showed up well in the photo, perhaps the photographer had been told to focus on that, though none of it was blurry, and Eleanor could clearly make out the double string of matched pearls and the rose shaped clasp.

It did not come as a surprise to see that Marjorie wore hers with the clasp on the left side of her neck, but her sisters had theirs on the right.

At least Eleanor now knew what she was looking for.

"Beautiful," she remarked, "both the three of you and the necklaces."

"Thank you." Marjorie took the photograph from Eleanor's outstretched hand, gave it a cursory glance, and twisting in her seat, placed it on a bookcase behind her chair. She turned back, a thoughtful look on her face.

"I'm sure the necklaces cost Father a lot of money, although he could well afford it. His idea was that we should think of them as family heirlooms."

"Do you ever regret selling yours?"

Marjorie shook her head. "No, never. It isn't my parents' fault that I'm the middle one of three, caught between the eldest and the baby. I tried not to resent it, that Barbara had everything before me and that the best was reserved for her. Then, when Amy became ill — consumption, you know — they lavished all their love, their energies, on her. I always seemed to be the forgotten one."

"It's often the way," Eleanor murmured. "I can understand your resentment."

"I'll admit I took it out on Barbara the most. That sort of one-sided treatment made me look for scapegoats and I could hardly blame poor Amy, especially with the comments Barbara began making when I started stepping out with, and then got engaged to, Geoffrey. I'm afraid we really fell out over that and I didn't invite her to our wedding."

"And you sold your necklace?"

"Yes."

"Do you remember who to?"

Marjorie put her cup down upon its saucer with a crash. "Don't tell me my sainted sister has sent you around here to buy it. What's happened to her own? Or does she just want two? Bah! What will she do then? Try and dig up the third?"

Eleanor bit back a gasp of surprise and annoyance. Perhaps she wasn't cut out for the role of an enquiry agent, after all. She had thought her question innocent enough and hadn't expected Marjorie to fly off the handle like she did. She had to admit that she was being intrusive, but how else to do the job?

"No, no, Mrs Arbuthnot," she said in a soft voice. "That is not the reason for my call. Please do not upset yourself."

Marjorie put her head in her hands and kneaded her forehead.

"I'm sorry, your Ladyship. Sometimes, just the mere mention of my sister is enough to make me feel hateful and murderous. I should not have snapped at you like that. Please forgive the appalling lapse in my behaviour."

"Not at all. It is I who should apologise for calling on you unannounced and asking questions on a subject clearly painful to you."

Marjorie gave a sudden bark of laughter as surprising, given the outburst that preceded it, as it was welcome. "A painful subject is a wonderful description of my sister, so you are doubly forgiven." She picked up her cup, saw that it was empty and put it down again. "Anyway, in answer to your question, I sold it back to the jeweller who made it. I can't now remember the name. I do recall that it was still in its box which had the initials GG upon it, and the shop was somewhere off Jermyn Street." She stopped and ran a forefinger across her lips. "No, it's gone. I'm sorry I can't be more specific than that."

Feeling that she had outstayed her welcome, Eleanor thanked her hostess and took her leave, no closer to laying her hands on Barbara's necklace than before.

Chapter 8

When her search for the jeweller responsible for crafting the three necklaces proved fruitless, Eleanor decided to have lunch in Simpson's in the Strand before driving back home.

She dropped the car off and walked around to the front of the building, where an attractive young man in his late twenties waited on the steps of Bellevue Mansions. He held the door open for her and swiftly followed her inside.

"Lady Eleanor Bakewell, is it? I wonder if you could spare me a few minutes? Danny Danvers, Daily Banner."

He thrust out a hand which Eleanor ignored.

"What do you want with me, Mr Danvers?"

"Oh, please, call me Danny. It's my readers, your ladyship. They want your story."

Eleanor raised a solitary eyebrow. "They do, do they?"

"Yes. You know, terror of the beautiful lady who discovered body of murdered newspaper proprietor. Oh yes, they'll lap that up. That's the sort of story they want."

He smiled in what he no doubt thought was a winning manner. It failed to win over Eleanor, who wanted nothing more than a strong drink and a modicum of peace and quiet.

"My mother always taught me that 'I want gets nothing'. Good day to you, Mr Danvers."

She turned on her heel, prepared to walk off and leave him in the lobby.

"Please, your ladyship. I could do with your help."

"What? To write scurrilous drivel? I don't think so."

"No, not that." He ran a hand down his cheek, and Eleanor noticed the haggard look around his eyes. "I need your help to clear my name. The police think I killed my boss."

Eleanor gave him a searching look. He didn't flinch.

It might be true, she reflected, and if it was then she stood to learn as much from him as he might from her. Just as long as her name did not appear all over the Daily Banner.

"All right," she said. "You'd better come up, but behave yourself. My maid is both armed, and a crack shot."

She opened the door with her key and went in. "I'm home, Tilly, and we have company."

Tilly hurried in, a smile of welcome on her round face as she took their coats.

"Take a seat, Mr Danvers. Can I get you a drink?"

"Thank you. A whisky, please." He pulled a reporter's notepad and a pencil from his jacket pocket and sat in the chair Eleanor had indicated.

As she fixed their drinks, Eleanor took stock of her guest. His slim torso and long limbs made him appear boyish and gangly, as if he had still to grow into his body. Under a mop of curly brown hair, eyes of the same colour surveyed the drawing room and appeared to find it to his liking. He relaxed in front of the fire, smiling in an open, almost impish fashion when she handed him his drink.

"Thank you."

Eleanor sat opposite and raised her own tumbler in salutation. "So, why do the police think you murdered Sir David Bristol, Mr Danvers?"

"Please call me Danny. Mr Danvers seems very formal." He crossed one leg over the other and took a pull of his drink. "I have a friend in this business who knows you. He said you weren't at all stand-offish, yet here I am feeling a little cowed."

Eleanor raised an eyebrow. She couldn't imagine anyone cowing the confident young man from the Daily Banner.

"And what friend might that be?"

"He's a chap by the name of Tommy Totteridge. He works for the Daily Clarion."

"Yes, I know Tommy." But did Totters, as he was known to close friends such as Eleanor, really know Danny Danvers, or was that young man chancing his luck? For now she would give him the benefit of the doubt, and make sure she checked with Tommy later.

"Well, there you are then."

"Yes, and still waiting for a reply to my question. Why do the police think you murdered your boss? What do they have to go on?"

Danvers didn't look so comfortable all of a sudden. He positively squirmed in his chair and with a quick nervous movement, took out a cigarette case. He opened it and offered it to Eleanor. She shook her head, waiting.

"I had a row with Bristol on the day of his death. He'd promised me that when the Banner's Chief Crime Reporter retired, which he is due to do at the end of this month, that I could step up and have his job." He lit his cigarette and blew smoke upwards.

"And?"

"And I discovered that the smarmy duplicitous worm had given the job to someone else, one of his cronies as it turns out."

That seemed unlikely. From what Eleanor knew of him, Sir David Bristol was not the sort to number reporters, even Chief Crime Reporters, among his friends. He was more likely to be found rubbing shoulders with the nobility or government ministers than hobnobbing with the sons of toil.

"That's hardly a reason to murder someone."

"Exactly." Danvers slapped one hand on his knee. "That's exactly what I told that pig-headed Chief Inspector, but he's disinclined to believe me, it seems."

Blount was no fool. He must have something to go on if he was making accusations. Unless Danvers was lying and using it as an excuse to worm his way into Eleanor's good graces.

"And what is it that you think I can do about that, Danny? Why have you come to me?"

"Because you found him." He looked sheepish. "I'm sorry, I wormed your name out of the manager at the Viceroy. I admit that was reprehensible on my part, but I needed to know more about Bristol's death than the police are letting on."

"So you can print it in your paper, with your byline and make a name for yourself? I don't think so."

"Nothing of the sort." He threw the remains of his cigarette into the fire. "You have a very low opinion of me for saying we've never met before."

With the exception of Tommy Totteridge, Eleanor did not think much of most journalists and reporters. She certainly wouldn't ascribe probity and self-sacrifice to anyone that worked for the more disreputable newspapers, and she counted the Daily Banner in that number. Besides, he had accosted her within her own building, inveigled his way into her home, and now sat drinking her whisky. Why should she trust him?

As if he had divined her thoughts, Danvers suddenly nodded. He leaned forward. "I know we reporters have a bad name — some, at least — and if any paper should have an exclusive on Bristol's murder, then it should surely be his own, but that isn't what I'm after. I am innocent of the man's murder, and I need to prove that to the chaps at Scotland Yard."

Was he really that naive? Eleanor wondered about his background and the length of time he'd been doing the job of crime reporter.

"Has it not occurred to you, that your very lack of knowledge about Sir David's killing, is proof enough that you had nothing to do with it?"

Danny squirmed in his chair and gulped more whisky. "Ah, well, you see, I'd told everyone in the office that I was going to have it out with him. I even asked there, and at the theatre, which box he was going to be in."

"Dear me, that was remarkably unfortunate."

"Yes, well, now Chief Inspector Blount's got to hear about it and thinks he's got me bang to rights for the murder. I wasn't even there."

"So, tell them where you were. Give them your alibi."

Danny blew out a long breath and ran a hand through his hair. "I can't. I haven't got one."

"Nonsense! You must have been somewhere."

Danvers admitted that he'd left the office in Fleet Street in a towering rage, sometime around nine o'clock that evening, intending to beard Bristol in his box at the Viceroy. Not having a car, he decided to walk and, at some point on his journey, began to cool down and think things through. He wandered, taking no heed of his surroundings, though aware he was approaching Covent Garden for in the distance he could hear the sound of what he assumed were traders arriving and departing, calling out to each other.

"Did you speak to anyone, or call in anywhere? A tobacconist or a public house, perhaps?"

"No, I just wandered, lost in my own thoughts. It's a wonder I didn't end up in the river, for I had no idea in which direction I headed."

"So, you never got to the Viceroy at all, then?"

A sheepish look settled on the handsome features. "I did as it happens, but by that time Sir David was long dead. I saw the policemen at the door, speaking to members of the audience as they came away. I nipped in and had a word with an usher, asking what was going off. When he told me, jeepers! I got out of there fast. I was so stunned, I didn't even think to get the story." He sighed. "Humph. Perhaps I'm not cut out to be Chief Crime Reporter after all. I hardly covered myself in glory."

He sat staring disconsolately into his whisky. Eleanor took pity on him.

"Well, you would merely have been first with the news that Bristol was dead, murdered, but you wouldn't have had much more of a story than that."

"So, what happened? The police have given very little away. How come you were there?"

"I went to see the play!"

"With Sir David?"

Exasperated, Eleanor shook her head. "No! I did not know the man. I just happened to be in the box next door and sitting right beside the party wall. Just before the end of the second act I thought I heard a bang or a heavy thump from next door and went to investigate."

"Hang on." Danvers' pen flew over the top sheet of his reporter's notebook, making a note of all Eleanor had said. He paused and gazed across at her. "You actually heard the shot, my lady?"

"Well, I heard something that sounded like one, yes, though my worry was that someone might have been taken ill and either collapsed or fallen."

"And you went to have a look. You're very brave."

"I think the word you are looking for is foolhardy."

Danvers laughed. "You said it. So, then what happened? You must have been awfully shocked."

"What happened? I told the manager to call the police. Look, Mr Danvers, I am not going to say how I felt or tell you my reactions. That has nothing to do with you — and if the Daily Banner makes up a cock-and-bull story that purports to be my words then I shall sue. I will also make sure that you, as well as your paper, are named in the action that I bring. Do I make myself clear?"

"Humph." His mouth twisted in disgust.

Eleanor didn't care. "In fact, if my name appears anywhere in your wretched report, I shall probably sue. However, should you care to write that an occupant of the next box found Sir David shot in the back of the head, and hurried to tell the manager and call the police, then I think all parties, you, your editor, your readers, and myself will be satisfied."

Danvers was frantically scribbling while she made her little speech. He looked up and said, "Thank you, my lady. All right, we have a deal. I won't print your name or mention you in any way. Now, is there anything else, any other details, you can give me?"

"Not really. I heard the noise about ten minutes to nine, or thereabouts, just before the end of the second act. I think, but only think, so don't go printing this as fact, that Bristol's killer must have opened the door, shot him from the doorway, closed it and walked away. There was no one around in the corridor when I left my box."

"Ah, but would you have seen them? The corridor is curved, and they could have been just out of your line of sight. And the Viceroy has decent carpets, so you wouldn't have heard them walking away, either."

He was right. Eleanor shivered as she realised how close she had come to seeing the killer.

Chapter 9

Sitting in the back of the taxi taking her to Clarice Montescue's twenty-fifth birthday party, Eleanor thought back over her interview with Danny Danvers, and kicked herself for not probing his knowledge of the Daily Banner's proprietor. If, as Major Armitage had suggested, Sir David Bristol had some questionable contacts, then the staff at the newspaper would be likely to know about it.

She had been that desperate to keep her name out of the newspapers that she had forgotten to make use of the handsome young reporter in the same manner he had tried to use her.

Shaking her head at her own shortcomings, and telling herself that she would remedy her oversight the next day, she alighted from the cab and walked through the open door of Montescue House.

She left her wrap with a footman and walked down the black and white tiled hall to the curved double staircase at the end.

"Eleanor! About time you got here. The fruit punch is excellent and running out fast."

Eleanor looked up to see Lady Ann Carstairs leaning over the first floor balustrade and waving a glass at her.

"Be careful you don't fall," she called back.

"Since when did you turn into my mother?"

Eleanor mounted the last few stairs and slipped her arm through her friend's. "Hello, darling. I see you didn't wait for me." She tapped Ann's glass.

"Sorry, old girl. Come and greet the birthday girl and then we can mingle. Totters and Sophie Westlake are already here and there's lots of others you'll know."

"Have you arranged this? Is it one of your parties?"

"Yes, and I managed to get hold of the best jazz band in London and hire them for the evening. Their trumpet player is marvellous, and as hot as his jazz."

Eleanor threw a keen glance at Ann. "Slept with him yet?"

"No, but I'm working on it."

The party was taking place in the house's Long Gallery which ran the entire width of the building and looked out over the square below. Luckily for Eleanor who wasn't overfond of jazz, the band were at the far end, while the bar lay not far from the double doors at the top of the staircase.

Clarice Montescue sat on a high stool, one elbow propped on the bar counter, as Eleanor arrived and wished her a happy birthday.

"Thank you, it's actually tomorrow and I intend to spend it in bed with a hangover."

"Good luck with that," Eleanor replied, as Ann passed her an overfilled glass.

She took a long pull on it to reduce the level, her mouth assailed by the flavour of strawberries and raw spirit. Her eyes watered.

"Didn't I tell you it was excellent?"

"You did, but one will be sufficient, I think."

She turned and rested her back against the counter and, with a quick, practised glance surveyed the room. For the most part she saw a familiar crowd — rich, titled, famous and infamous — though there were a few new faces.

"Who's the tall gent leaning against the chimney breast over there? To the right of the fireplace. Not sure I know him."

"That's Gerry Hope-Weedon, a government minister and the up-and-coming man, I hear. He's not been in London long."

Recalling the name from Barbara Lancashire's list, Eleanor nodded. He was also one of the three men of interest to Major Armitage, but she ignored that fact. She had to focus on her own job, not his.

"Then I'd like an introduction, please."

Ann gave her friend a sharp glance. "He takes your fancy, does he?"

Eleanor laughed. "In a manner of speaking."

They navigated their way across the vast space of the Gallery, weaving between gaily clad girls in colourful dresses dripping with jewels. So many of them sported feather-waving headbands that Eleanor was reminded of a visit to the bird house at London Zoo.

At one point Ann told Eleanor to stay close and not get lost.

"Don't worry. I know where I'm going. I was in the Girl Guides," she joked.

When they eventually reached their quarry he was talking to Tommy Totteridge and Sophie Westlake, which made the introductions easier.

"Eleanor, old girl!" exclaimed Tommy. "You're looking good. How the deuce are you?"

"Fine, thank you." She touched cheeks with first Tommy, then Sophie, and stood back turning her gaze on the new man.

At Tommy's introduction, Gerald Hope-Weedon bowed low over her hand.

"Delighted to make your acquaintance, Lady Eleanor."

He had a shock of blond hair over the palest blue eyes that Eleanor had ever seen. Undoubtedly attractive, with an athletic figure and a strong jaw and high cheek bones, she thought he could have stepped straight down from a plinth in some ancient Greek temple.

"Likewise," she replied.

His eyes locked onto hers and held her gaze. She only broke away when she realised that Tommy was talking animatedly beside her.

"I'd just collared Gerry here, because he's an MP newly arrived in London, and with a ministerial position to boot. Now that I'm a journalist, I thought we could do a feature on him."

"I thought you were the Arts correspondent, Totters."

Tommy's round face lit up. "Yes, so I am, but I'm willing to have a go at anything to improve my all round skills. Besides, Gerry and I go way back."

Eleanor laughed. "Don't tell me you were at school together."

"Totters went to school with everybody, didn't you, my sweet?" Sophie gave a playful punch to his arm.

"Actually, no. We belong to the same club."

Eleanor's glance lingered on Hope-Weedon's physique for a fraction longer than was seemly. "A sports club? I didn't know you played sport, Totters. You would have made an excellent rugby player."

Totteridge blushed. "I meant White's Club."

Eleanor nodded. White's was the oldest gentleman's club in London. Situated in St James's Street, many considered it the most exclusive private club in the capital.

"Oh, I see. Not a sports club, then."

The three women laughed at Tommy's obvious discomfiture, until Eleanor put out a hand and apologised. He was a very old and dear friend.

"I'm sorry. I shouldn't tease you." She turned to Hope-Weedon. "How long have you been a member there? Is it as expensive as they claim?"

"Membership certainly isn't cheap, my lady, but if you were thinking of applying —"

"No no, of course not. I'm well aware that it is for gentlemen only."

But if Hope-Weedon was a member of the Labour Party, a party that represented the working classes, how did he square his political views with being a member of an expensive place like White's? It would be rude to ask, but the question gnawed away at her.

She was so engrossed in her thoughts that it took her a moment to realise that Tommy had asked that very question.

"So, how come you joined the Labour Party then, Hoppers? I should have thought the Conservatives would have been a better fit for you?"

Eleanor hid a smile at Tommy's way of shortening everyone's name — a relic from his days at a public school where it happened to all the pupils and he himself had been dubbed with the name 'Totters'. Gerald Hope-Weedon didn't appear to be too pleased by it, though. He wrinkled his nose as if a bad smell had wafted beneath it. Eleanor thought he'd got off lightly — he might have ended up with the epithet 'Weeders' or 'Weedy'.

"I had my reasons," he said, with a condescending air. "A man's politics are his own affair, don't you know."

Eleanor hated pomposity of any kind. She wished she had a special pin with which to puncture it. Ridicule would usually do the trick, but now was not the time to use it. She could not afford to alienate the man when she still had things to learn.

"Now that you're in government, you must have come across Sir Robert Lancashire," she said. "Did you enjoy his wife's soirée the other evening?"

Hope-Weedon blinked at her a few times, fluttering sandy lashes so pale as to be almost invisible. "I didn't see your ladyship there. I'm sure I would have remembered if I did."

"No, I wasn't there, but Barbara, Sir Robert's wife, told me all about it."

"Did she tell you how ghastly it was? I was never so bored in all my life. I wish you had have been there, you know. You would have livened it up immensely.

Eleanor noted the twinkle in his eye, while beside her Ann coughed. "I need another drink," she said. "Anyone else?"

"Yes, I'll come with you." Sophie detached herself from Tommy's side. "I need to talk to you anyway."

"Umm...perhaps I should go and get another drink as well," said Tommy.

"No you don't." Eleanor baulked at the idea of being alone with Hope-Weedon — his last comment had been rather too forward for her taste — and grabbed Tommy's arm. "I need a chaperone. Besides, Sophie will get you a drink while she's at the bar, and I need to ask you something."

"Oh? What's that?"

"Do you know Danny Danvers of the Daily Banner?"

"Ah." Tommy grimaced and looked down at his feet, but Eleanor also sensed that Hope-Weedon had tensed at the name.

"Good grief, Totters, old man," he said, "don't say you know that little oik?"

"Little oik, Mr Hope-Weedon? That seems a trifle unkind for saying that the Daily Banner appears to be your Party's mouthpiece of late." Eleanor stared up into the pale blue eyes. "And Danny Danvers is, after all, a working man."

"Yes, Gerry. What's your beef with Danvers? Has he been after you for your story, too? He's not a bad bloke, but you really would be better off giving me the interview, you know."

Annoyed that Tommy had wriggled out of things and changed the subject, Eleanor gritted her teeth. He had at least answered the question by his shame-faced reaction to it. Danvers had told the truth about the two of them discussing her and she shivered at the thought of being talked about behind her back — and by Tommy of all people. Still, at least he'd said something nice about her.

"There is no story, Totters. I'm just an average chap with no secrets for journalists to uncover. I support the rights of the working man, yes even Danvers, I suppose, though I don't care for the fellow. Your readers wouldn't want to read about me. They'd be bored silly within a sentence or two. Wait until I've made my mark in government, and come and talk to me then."

He looked remarkably smug for one who had only so recently been elected.

"Are you so sure that you will make a mark, Mr Hope-Weedon?"

He nodded, lips twisted into an ugly sneer. "Oh, I think so, Lady Eleanor. I think it's written in my stars, and believe me, I aim to follow that star. You'll see."

"Good luck, then. It will mean getting your name and presence known more widely than it is now."

"Yes, I'm aware of that."

"It will also mean listening to the people, talking to them, even if it means throwing your pearls before swine." She saw him blench at the phrase. "I shall follow your career with interest."

She nodded to both the men, then turned on her heel and went to join Ann who was still at the bar. Sophie, she was told, had gone to find the amenities.

"You'll never guess," Ann said, as Eleanor asked for another glass of punch.

Eleanor looked at her friend who appeared to be jiggling with suppressed excitement. "Guess what?"

"Totters and Sophie are getting engaged and they've asked me to organise the party."

"Oh, that's wonderful news, and on both counts." Eleanor beamed at her friend. "I always knew she'd get her man and Sophie will be very good for him and make him an excellent wife."

"Yes, she's just told me, and although it won't be for another couple of weeks, when the families have been told and the official announcement made, they are having a small get-together for friends at Tommy's place the day after tomorrow. We are both invited and Sophie asked me to pass it on and let you know, but remember it's hush-hush at the moment."

Eleanor checked her mental diary. "Oh, I shall definitely be there," she said, "and I look forward to it, though I won't say the same if Gerald Hope-Weedon is also invited."

"No," agreed Ann, casting a glance across the room. "That man is dangerous. I'd stay well away, if I were you."

Chapter 10

"Is that you, Lady Eleanor? It's Barbara Lancashire, here. I wonder if you would come and see me, immediately if that is possible, but otherwise at your earliest convenience."

It was still early and Eleanor, surprised by the peremptory voice, almost said no. However, she had nothing else on her agenda that morning, and if it meant an opportunity to drive the Lagonda, she might as well accept the summons.

Barely twenty minutes later she stood in front of Lady Lancashire, feeling rather as a naughty schoolboy might feel in front of a teacher with a cane, and wondered what had got her client so het up.

She had to wait, though, while Barbara spoke first to the butler who had shown Eleanor in.

"Have you seen to his lordship's evening suit, Harvey? I can't have him going around with holes in his jacket, like some common beggar. Please tell the valet to get rid of it and phone the tailor to come and measure him up for a new one."

"Very good, my lady."

He bowed himself out and gave Eleanor an apologetic look which she acknowledged with a brief nod. He was not to blame for his mistress's rudeness.

Barbara at last turned her attention to her visitor.

"Thank you for coming so promptly, your ladyship. I thought it best to tell you this in person rather than over the telephone, but I'm happy to say that I no longer require your services. Tell me how much I owe you and I'll settle up."

She moved to the walnut bureau under the window, leaving Eleanor staring after her, open mouthed upon the carpet.

"Have you found your necklace, then?" she asked, when she trusted herself to speak.

She couldn't imagine that the thief had returned it — thieves seldom had an attack of conscience sufficient to repent and return what they had taken. Had it never been stolen in the first place? Or merely misplaced? That seemed unlikely given Barbara's detailed account of the discovery of her loss, but how else to account for her own summary dismissal.

For that was what it felt like — and on her very first professional assignment, too.

Eleanor's mouth filled with the bitter taste of defeat.

"What?" Barbara turned back from the bureau with her cheque book in her hand.

"I asked if you'd found your necklace."

"Oh, yes. Ha ha!" She gave a loud brittle laugh that sounded totally false. As false as the smile on her red-painted lips. "So stupid of me. It had completely slipped my mind until first thing this morning that I had sent them for cleaning." She gave a tight-lipped smile. "So, in what amount should I make out my cheque?"

Eleanor was in two minds whether to name some outrageous sum or not, but if she did, would not put it past Lady Lancashire to tell her friends that she had been overcharged and the task not even accomplished. For the sake of any future business, she must be generous now.

"No, that's all right, Lady Lancashire. Although I did make some enquiries, I did not find your pearls and accepting a fee now would feel as if I was taking money from you under false pretences. I'm just delighted that you have found them."

Beaming at this outcome, Barbara snapped shut her cheque book. "Yes, it's not as if you did anything to earn a fee, I suppose, but your attitude is to be commended."

Eleanor clamped her jaws closed until struck by a sudden thought. "If they are back from the jewellers, do you think I might see the pearls? They sounded so beautiful when you described them to me, and I have a particular fondness for pearls myself."

In an instant, Lady Lancashire's air of bonhomie vanished. Eleanor felt the temperature of the air between them drop by several degrees.

"I'm afraid not, my lady. Some other time perhaps. I'm in a hurry to go out."

She wasn't dressed for going out. Her woollen day dress had seen better days and her hair needed attention; wisps of it hung down from the bun on the back of her head. She rang the bell at the side of the fire, and said a brief good-bye when the butler arrived to show Eleanor out.

In no time at all she was standing back on the pavement.

"Well," Eleanor murmured, as she started the Lagonda. "It's a wonder she didn't chase me off the premises."

She didn't pull away from Eaton Square immediately, but sat thinking over the interview. If Barbara Lancashire was once again in possession of her pearls, then Eleanor was a Dutchman. Sent them for cleaning and only just remembered? Bah!

"Barbara must think me a fool, if she believes I swallowed that ridiculous story."

Why the woman would lie, she had no idea, yet Eleanor was certain that she had. Barbara still didn't have her pearls, a fact proved by her refusal to show them, so what had happened to make her revoke the commission she had given only two days previously?

Unable to fathom Lady Lancashire's odd behaviour, Eleanor gave up trying.

With no other plans for the morning, she decided to call in at Bakewell House on the way home. She would return with Tilly in a day or so, but might as well go over the house now, and make sure that all was well first.

The Lagonda purred along as it carried her through Mayfair and into a stately old square with its central garden filled with neat beds and plane trees. Their bare branches cast a tracery of shadows on the ground beneath and a small child ran along between them, playing hide and seek with its mother.

The London home of the Duke of Bakewell occupied a near central position on the south side of Berkeley Square. Eleanor drew up against the kerb and looked at the door, its black paint grimy and dusty, the steps up to it littered with russet leaves. To either side the boarded-up windows gazed sightlessly back at her.

Such a shame, she thought. So many of the houses in the square had been sold, the families no longer able to afford them, or having no one to bequeath them to after the war. In the circumstances, leaving Bakewell House to fall into rack and ruin seemed almost a criminal act.

It was a huge property, rising to four floors, and attics above that. Unfortunately, it needed a huge family, employing an army of staff, both to fill it and to ensure its smooth running. Even so, she hoped her father had no plans to sell it. Eleanor might even be prepared to give up her snug little roost at Bellevue Mansions if it meant being able to keep the house, with all its history and its memories, occupied.

She walked up the steps, slipped her key into the lock and stepped into the darkened interior. Everything lay shrouded and covered in dust cloths and she picked her way warily down the hall with only the light from the transom over the door to guide her. The fuses had been removed and no lights were working. She made a mental note to bring a couple of torches with her, when she came back with Tilly.

The air smelt musty and stale and seemed to settle over her, wrapping her in silence. It took a deal of effort not to tiptoe.

At the end of the hall she put out a hand to the door into the servants' quarters, groping for it in the darkness. A swing door, it opened both ways without a handle or knob and she pushed gently and peered beyond.

In contrast to the hall, the kitchen was dark, but candles and matches had been left on a table in the centre of the room. She crossed the floor, one hesitant step at a time, hands held out in front of her, unsure where the other furniture might be and anxious not to bark her shins against benches and chairs.

She groped around for the candles in their holders and quickly lit first one and then the other. By their flickering light, she gazed around, looking for the fuse box. She could not see one, and hoped that Tilly knew where it was. The idea of going throughout the house with only the light of candles or torches to guide them, did not appeal and she shivered in the cool air and nearly dropped the candle.

The air in the kitchen was fresh! What's more, of the three remaining candles on the table, two were little more than stubs.

She hurried to the back door and found it locked and with no sign of the key. The hook upon which the key normally hung was empty. The windows, like those at the front, were shuttered and secure. Eleanor put her hands against the boards, but could feel no draught.

Standing with her back to the door she held the candle at arm's length and stared at its unflickering flame.

"That's odd."

She didn't stay in the house for much longer. An unwelcome feeling of apprehension saw her blow out the candle and make her way back down the hallway and out the front door.

When she arrived back at Bellevue Mansions, Tilly attempted to raise her mistress's spirits by serving hot coffee and telling her not to worry.

"There's probably fresh air getting in through the chimney. If you saw no sign of a break-in —"

"I didn't, but fresh air can't light and burn candles. Somebody's been in there, I'm sure of it. I wasn't prepared to check the rest of the house to see if anyone was there , or anything had been stolen, without proper light to see by. Not on my own, anyway, so I came home."

"Did you unlock the back door with your key, and check outside?"

Eleanor shook her head and reached for the cigarette box on the mantelpiece. "No, I never thought to. I think I was too surprised to think straight and, if I'm honest, my mind was still engaged trying to work out what Barbara Lancashire was up to."

"Oh? What happened there, then?"

Eleanor reported her interview with her erstwhile client. "I can't say that I'm not relieved that I don't have to go around asking Barbara's guests if they stole her pearls. It wasn't quite the sort of thing I expected to be doing when I started this detecting malarkey, and it may call for a rethink. Either way, I'm sure she hasn't got her necklace back, just as I'm sure she never sent it for cleaning."

"Why would she lie about it, though, my lady?"

Eleanor shrugged, arms wide. "I'm blessed if I know." She lit her cigarette. "I can think of any number of reasons why she might have got rid of the necklace herself, but in that case she wouldn't have called me in."

"Unless she wanted you as proof that it had been stolen, rather than pawned, say."

"Ye gods!" Eleanor stared at her maid, and let out a whistle. "I wish I'd got your devious and clever mind, old girl. That hadn't occurred to me."

Tilly sniffed. "You did say that she gambled, didn't you?"

"Yes, so her sister told me, and Penelope Studley-Gore did, as well. You could be on to something, there. If Barbara had run up gambling debts, then she may well have pawned, or even sold the necklace to pay them." She tapped her fingers on the arm of her chair. "Then what?"

"Does it matter? Now that she's said she doesn't want you to try and get them back?"

"I suppose not, but I can't say that I'm happy to have my services dispensed with so soon after receiving the commission. It's barely more than forty-eight hours. What happened in the meantime, eh? It may not matter — but I still want to know. Besides, it goes against the grain to be used like that, and by Barbara Lancashire of all people."

Chapter 11

Dismissing Lady Lancashire, Eleanor told Tilly she was going out again. "I shan't be long. I'm only going to the Post Office on the corner. I need to get a greeting card and post it."

With this chore completed she walked back home, her mind returning to thoughts of jewel thefts and Barbara Lancashire's abrupt change of heart. She had almost reached Bellevue Mansions when she heard a thin cry. Further along the pavement stood a newsboy.

"Get your mornin' paper! Daily Banner!"

Eleanor approached him.

"Mornin' paper, Miss?" He held out a copy in a grimy hand, black with newsprint.

"What's your name, young man?"

"Joe, Miss, Joe Minshull. Daily Banner!" He continued to shout his wares.

Eleanor looked down at him. His greasy dark hair flopped into one eye and his head constantly turned, this way and that, as he looked for customers. His newsboy's bag, stuffed with papers, pulled heavily on one shoulder making him appear crooked.

"I'm Lady Eleanor Bakewell, Joe. Do you regularly come to this part of Piccadilly?"

He craned his head back to gaze up at her. "Coo! A toff, are yer? Yeah, I'm often around this way. Twice a day, usually, three times sometimes if there's a midday edition. Get your mornin' paper!"

"Have you ever seen anyone hanging around the front of this building?" She pointed to the wide shallow steps behind them. "Bellevue Mansions."

A cough shook his thin frame. "Can't say as I 'ave, my lady."

She crouched beside him, so that they were eye to eye. "Would you like to do a job for me, Joe?"

He sniffed and peered at her, the pointed nose in the pale face quivering with suspicion. "Job?" he asked. "What sort of job?" He shivered again in his thin, frayed jacket, his body swaying.

Eleanor put an arm around the narrow waist to steady him. "When did you last eat, Joe?"

He shook his head. "Daily Banner!"

"Never mind that. You're coming with me."

"Nah, Miss. Gotta sell me papers."

Eleanor rose, transferring her grip to his shoulder. "Then I'll buy the lot of them. Come on."

She ignored his protests, although she almost had to drag him up the steps. The look on the astonished doorman's face was nothing compared to the reception she received from Tilly.

"Cor, lumme, my lady. What have you brought home now?"

"A secret weapon, quite possibly, but first he needs feeding up and a hot drink, please."

Tilly wrinkled her nose. "He looks as if a bath might do him some good as well."

"All in good time, though I should let him wash his hands and face in the scullery."

Faced with the indomitable will of his benefactress — or maybe his captor, Joe's face suggested he wasn't sure which — he was led off, too weary to complain.

Eleanor took her usual seat by the fireside, smiling quietly to herself at the sounds — Tilly's chuntering and the boy's answering yells — emanating from the scullery.

Had she done the right thing in bringing him home? From a humanitarian point of view, undoubtedly — the boy was undernourished, possibly ill, and certainly in need of some care — and, if he was prepared to take it, she did have a job for young Joe. One that, with any luck, would benefit both of them.

She shrugged. Only time would tell if she was right about that.

When he returned after half an hour his face and hands were cleaner, his hair had been combed and a smile of sheer bliss hovered around his mouth — together with a smear of marmalade, if Eleanor were any judge.

"Thank you, my lady, thank you Miss Tilly. I wish I could have a breakfast like that every day."

"Come in and sit down, Joe."

She indicated the chair opposite, noting the way Tilly's eyebrows rose, but before the maid had a chance to voice her objections, Joe sat, cross-legged, on the carpet before the fire.

"Do you have family?" Eleanor asked him.

"Yeah, me mum and a younger brother, but my mum's sick and can't work."

"Oh? I'm sorry to hear that. Is it anything serious?"

He shrugged. "Influenza, I think." For a moment he looked worried, then gave another shrug and got the conversation back on track. "You said you was gonna buy all my newspapers, my lady."

"And I am." Eleanor picked up her purse. "How much do I owe you?"

Joe's eyes widened and his fingers and mouth moved rapidly. "There's twelve copies there at tuppence each, so I makes that two shillin'."

"So do I." Eleanor counted out the coins and passed them across. "Now, you have to pay that to the newspapers, but how would you like to earn some money of your own?"

His eyes grew wary. "What would I 'ave to do?"

"Do you always sell your papers around here?"

"Yeah. This is my patch."

"Does it also cover Berkeley Square?"

"Well, sort of." He scratched an ear. "Don't sell much there, though. They're all Times people around there."

That made sense. Most occupants of the Square would consider the Daily Banner beneath them, fit only for the servants to read.

"Well, I'd like you to keep your eyes and ears open, both here and at a particular house in Berkeley Square, and report to me what you see."

Joe twisted his hands in his lap. "Sounds easy enough, but I ain't doing anything criminal. Don't hold with that. I 'spects you don't either, being a lady, an' all that."

He sounded hopeful and Eleanor smiled to put him at ease.

"Very much so, young man. In fact, I fight crime, and that's where this job comes in."

"Oh, yeah?" His look suggested he didn't believe a word of it.

"Listen, Joe. Did you know that the man who owned the Daily Banner, Sir David Bristol, was murdered recently?"

"Yeah, I heard about that, all right. They was all talking about it down the delivery office."

"Well, I found his body at the theatre."

"Cor!"

"As a result, there are an awful lot of people who keep pestering me, mainly reporters. I've already had to send Danny Danvers off with a flea in his ear."

Joe grinned. "I'd 'ave liked to seen that. Ol' Danny's a real hard nut."

Perhaps he appeared that way to a boy like Joe. Eleanor had thought the reporter a bit of a softie.

"So, whenever you are down this end of Piccadilly with your papers, will you take note of any men you see hanging around? I don't expect you to get their names, but a description would be useful."

The boy rubbed a finger down the bridge of his nose. "Yeah, I reckon I could do that, but 'ow would I let you know if I seen anybody lurking?"

"Come inside and speak to the doorman. Tell him your name and ask him to ring up to this flat. Tilly or I will then come down and get the details from you. I'll let the doorman know that you might call and that he is to let me know when you do, so you won't have to worry about him telling you to clear off."

Joe held a reddened hand towards the fire. He seemed lost in thought, staring at the flames as they flickered and danced, and said nothing in reply.

"So, will you take the job on, Joe? I'll pay you a shilling every time you report something — assuming your information proves accurate, that is. Here's a shilling in advance and to show my good faith."

Eleanor took another coin from her purse and held it out to him. She had no way to be sure if Joe Minshull would also act in good faith, or whether he would turn up every day with some made up story about suspicious characters lurking around Bellevue Mansions, but if she showed that she trusted him he might be less inclined to try and fool her.

The shilling waited in her hand. To her surprise, he made no move to take it from her.

Eventually, he took his gaze from the fire, glanced at the coin, then raised his eyes to her face.

"Please, my lady, you can keep your money if there's any chance I could be paid in Miss Tilly's bacon and egg breakfasts instead."

Eleanor's eyes widened. She looked across at her maid, playing chaperone by standing in front of the kitchen door, and saw her eyes widen, too. Then Tilly gave a long slow shake of her head — a shake that Eleanor interpreted not in the negative, but as an expression of despair that a boy could get so hungry as to pass up on a shiny new shilling. The shake was followed by a quick nod.

"All right with me," Tilly said. "But next time you come, Joe Minshull, you'll have a bath before you eat."

Joe's head shot around to look at her. "Aw, miss."

"Don't worry. We do have hot water and you needn't think I'm going to bath you, so you can preserve your modesty." She gave a loud sniff.

Eleanor leaned forward. "What do you say, Joe? And I'll still give you a shilling, too."

He beamed and started pinching the skin on his forearm. "I ain't dreaming, am I?"

"No," said Tilly, before Eleanor could respond. "And you'll do what you've promised to do and behave yourself while you're here, otherwise you'll find I've got more than one use for a rolling pin."

Thinking the threat to be real, Joe cowered. "Yes, Miss Tilly."

He took the shilling from Eleanor and his empty newspaper bag from the floor and Tilly walked downstairs with him and showed him out.

When he had gone, Eleanor wondered again if she had done the right thing. The thought that she might have put the paperboy in danger never crossed her mind, though it was to come back and haunt her in the days ahead.

Chapter 12

Later that morning a knock at the front door disturbed Eleanor as she sat in the small room she used as a study, making notes on the Lancashire case. When the sound of muffled voices reached her, she slipped the sheet of paper into the desk drawer and out of sight.

"Miss Deanna Dacre to see you, my lady." The maid's face was deadpan. "She's in the drawing room."

"Thank you, Tilly. I'll be right there. Would you make a pot of coffee for our guest, please?"

The actress sat on the sofa. She was dressed completely in black, from her mid calf length skirt to the hat on her head. Her eyes were obscured by the hat's net veil, though the lips beneath were painted scarlet.

Thus she might have looked had she been dressed by a wardrobe mistress in order to play the role of a grieving widow. But Deanna Dacre was not a widow and Eleanor felt a certain disgust that she was expected to view, and presumably treat, her as one.

At Eleanor's approach, Deanna lifted the veil and offered her hand.

"I hope you don't mind me calling unannounced like this, my lady. I got your name from Chief Inspector Blount of Scotland Yard. He told me you found...David."

"I did." Eleanor indicated that the actress should resume her seat and walked past to her own chair by the fireside.

"And that it was you who called the police?"

Eleanor heard the question in the voice and answered it. "Strictly speaking that was the theatre manager, after I'd informed him of the...tragedy. He called the police, not I."

Deanna fluttered her long dark eyelashes. "Oh, well, it amounts to the same thing."

Wondering at the real reason behind the visit, Eleanor remained silent. Deanna Dacre would tell her in her own good time. In the meantime, Eleanor smiled in a way that she hoped would inspire confidence and waited.

"Lady Eleanor, I..."

"Yes, Miss Dacre?"

Deanna's mouth curved briefly. She looked apologetic when she began again. "If it isn't too painful, or an imposition, would you tell me what happened?"

"There's nothing to tell, really. I was in the box next door to Sir David, and heard what I thought was a bang, so went to investigate."

Deanna leaned forward. "And?" she urged.

Was this mere prurience on Deanna's part? Or did something deeper lie behind the desire to know what Eleanor had seen and heard?

"And, sadly, I found him dead. He had been shot at close range in the back of the head and lay slumped forward over the edge of the box."

"Oh!" As if by magic, a wisp of cotton appeared out of the actress's sleeve and went to her mouth, though not, Eleanor noted, close enough to smudge the lipstick. A sob escaped her. "My poor David."

Luckily, Tilly brought in the coffee at that moment, preventing Eleanor from uttering the scathing retort that had risen to her lips.

"Thank you, Tilly. Leave it here, will you?" She patted the small table at her side, and gave a one-shouldered shrug in answer to the maid's raised eyebrow. She would talk about it later when their visitor had gone.

"Please help yourself to cream and sugar," Eleanor said, as she passed a cup of aromatic arabica to her guest. "Perhaps then you'd like to tell me the real reason you are here."

"Oh." Deanna took a sip of coffee. "I really did want to know what you saw. I take it there was no one else in Sir David's box?"

Was that what lay behind her visit, behind her questions? Jealousy?

Eleanor answered honestly, if a little warily. "No one, nor did I see any sign that he'd had company." She gazed shrewdly at the actress. "Except for his murderer, of course."

The comment did not have the effect that Eleanor had expected. Deanna merely nodded and sipped more coffee.

"Lady Eleanor, a mutual acquaintance — I won't mention the name — has told me that you have recently set up as a private enquiry agent. Is that right?"

Eleanor felt a familiar sinking feeling. Once again she sensed that a mighty hand was forcing her onto a path she did not wish to take. Only with an effort of will did she keep the smile on her face. "Yes, that's correct."

"Then, I'd like to ask you to investigate Sir David's death. I want to know who killed my patron and the play's benefactor. I don't care how much you want — one hundred, five hundred, name your price — but I must know who killed him."

Unlike many of her class, Eleanor did not consider the discussion of money to be sordid, and because money was not the reason she enquired into things, she waved Deanna's offer aside for the moment.

"Why come to me, Miss Dacre? The police are perfectly capable, you know."

"Then you have greater faith in them than I do. Besides, I cannot rely on them to be discreet."

"I see. You do realise, don't you, that if I take on this case, it will be to discover the truth and to bring the culprit to justice. Any unpalatable or damaging facts will not be swept under the carpet and, if I do find out who is guilty, I will inform the police and not just yourself."

Deanna nodded. "Yes, I suppose you would have to do that."

"I could not do anything else. Also, are you prepared for me to ask some impertinent and personal questions? I will have to do so to get at the truth. Were it not for the fact that you were on stage at the time, you might be a suspect, yourself."

Deanna grimaced. "The police certainly treated me as one."

Another reason for the actress to ask Eleanor to investigate?

"I can assure you that I will treat your answers as confidences as far as I may, where I feel that they are not germane to the investigation, that is."

"Yes, I have nothing to hide."

Eleanor wondered if that were true.

"Very well, then. You described Sir David as your patron. Was he more than that? Was there a more...intimate relationship between you?"

The actress put her cup and saucer on the tray and sat back. She smoothed down the skirt over her knee and a sad expression appeared on her face. "Yes, there was. David only consented to invest money in the play if I became his mistress."

Eleanor's eyebrows rose. Was the woman prepared to sell herself in order to become a star?

"Oh dear. Have I shocked you?" Deanna gave a tinkling laugh. "We artists aren't as louche as all that, you know, and besides he was not unattractive and we shared an interest in the arts."

"No, I'm not shocked. How long had you known him?"

"About six months. I met him at a party and we got talking. We went out together a few times, and I had hoped for a more permanent relationship. I thought I'd found a kindred spirit, but when we became lovers, it was obvious that David didn't see things the same way."

She spoke quite freely. Eleanor reminded herself that the woman on the sofa was an actress. Had she rehearsed these words, expecting to be asked probing and personal questions?

"Have you any idea who might want to kill him? Was he the sort who had enemies?"

Deanna ran a forefinger below her lower lip.

"I have no one particular in mind, but there were many, I think, that resented him. They resented his power and his wealth. Then there were some who disapproved of his ennoblement. I've heard it said that he only received a knighthood because he put money into the government's coffers."

"Did he do that?"

"I don't know. It wasn't something we talked about, and he became Sir David long before we met. He certainly supported the government, and at one time he used the Daily Banner to endorse their policies. It was staunchly Conservative."

In the normal run of things, Eleanor paid little attention to politics and, although she came from a wealthy and privileged background often found herself more in sympathy with socialist than with conservative thinking. It was a viewpoint she kept to herself.

"Was?" she asked. "I tend not to read newspapers. Has the Banner changed its allegiance?"

The actress lifted her hands and spread them. "I believe it has become more...um...populist, I think that was the term David used, and not everybody approved of that. As far as he was concerned it sold more newspapers, and thus made him more money. He was all for that."

Surprised at the sneer on Deanna's beautiful face, Eleanor pressed her about the state of her relationship with the murdered man.

"You sound as though you didn't like him much."

Deanna screwed up her nose and moved uncomfortably on her seat. "Let's just say that there had been a cooling off on both sides. Sir David Bristol was not the man I took him to be when we first met. Lately, I'd come to think of him as having a shady side."

"Shady?" Eleanor poured more coffee for them both. "In what way?"

"It's hard to explain. There were certain phone calls that he made and people that came to his house and, if I were there, he would either banish me to another room, or even order a taxi and send me away. Thank you." She took the refilled cup and added cream.

Eleanor did the same with her own coffee and asked, "These people, were they connected with his business?"

"He said so, and that I would find it boring, but he would never quite meet my eye, and I sensed he was lying to me, covering up the real reason. There were times when he would spend the whole weekend at his house in Windsor. It's a beautiful place, on the banks of the Thames quite close to Windsor Castle, but on those occasions he would never invite me."

"You did go to Windsor with him sometimes, though?"

"Oh, yes." She let out that tinkling laugh again. "I once accused him of having another mistress there."

A natural assumption, Eleanor thought, considering what Penelope had told her about the Countess Vera Ivanova in Menton. Perhaps Sir David Bristol collected beautiful women like some men collected works of art.

"Did you ever find out if he had?"

Deanna shook her head. "No. He denied it, and when I jestingly said that I might turn up and catch him with her, he became very aggressive."

"Oh? In what way?"

"He grabbed hold of my face in one hand and squeezed hard. "He said that if I ever did, I would live to regret it." She shivered. "I believed him. His eyes blazed and he was clearly furious. I was terrified."

"Had you not seen his temper before then?"

"No, never. I had to go on stage that night wearing extra make-up to cover the bruises, but when he collected me at the stage-door to take me for supper that evening, he was all sweetness and full of apologies. He even brought me roses."

"Forgive me for asking, Miss Dacre, but given the cooling in your relationship, why are you so anxious to know who killed Sir David?"

Deanna turned a beseeching gaze upon her hostess. "Because I still cared." She leaned forward, hands clasped at her breast, and in a voice full of anguish and emotion said, "Don't you see? Despite what he had done, I still cared. Please tell me you will investigate. Please."

Eleanor, ignoring the histrionics and the pinprick of doubt that insinuated itself into her thoughts, suppressed a sigh. "Very well, Miss Dacre. I'll see what I can find out. I will be in touch."

Chapter 13

After the actress had departed, Eleanor fetched her notebook from where she had left it on the study desk and began to jot down her thoughts and make a record of the conversation that had just taken place.

Did she believe the reason the actress had given for wanting Eleanor to look into Bristol's death? Not entirely, although she had agreed to do so. Now that she was no longer required to look for Barbara Lancashire's pearls, she had no other commission on her books and could afford the time to take a closer look at Sir David's murder.

She stopped writing when she came to the part where the actress had talked of her lover's business dealings and sat back, tapping her fingers on the table. Should she inform Major Armitage of these details? They sounded the sort of thing he'd like to know about, secret meetings and shady goings-on, and it was up to him to decide whether they were relevant or not.

She toyed with the idea of picking up the phone and calling him, but the hunger to hear his voice that suddenly surged through her kept Eleanor in her chair.

"Don't be such a fool."

Eleanor carried on with her notes and when, an hour or so later, she did pick up the phone, it was to place a call to Ann Carstairs.

"Hi, Ann, it's Eleanor."

"Ooh, ooh, don't shout," her friend protested, though Eleanor's voice had been at its normal level. "Have some consideration for a girl with a bad head."

"Hangover, huh? It serves you right."

"Beast. What did I ever do to deserve an uncaring friend like you?"

Eleanor laughed. "My, we are feeling sorry for ourselves, aren't we, darling? Look, are you busy today?"

"Moderately so, my lamb, or I will be in a bit, once I've got the right head on. I've got a lot of calls to make for Sophie and Totter's party, and I picked up another commission for a bash at the Connaught. Why do you ask?"

"I was wondering what you remember about the night we went to see *The Burning Heart* at the Viceroy."

"Other than you going in search of a dead body, you mean?"

"Ann!" Eleanor heard the laugh followed by the groan at the other end of the line.

"Don't shout."

"I won't if you behave yourself. Please tell me what you remember, and leave all references to dead men out of it."

"Oh, all right. Well, Deanna Dacre was fabulous, what a performance! What a star!"

Eleanor considered the performance that had taken place in her drawing room earlier, and had to agree, but it wasn't Ann's opinion of the play, or its leading actress, that she was after.

"She was. I've just had her around here, as a matter of interest. I'll fill you in on that some other time," she said, in answer to her friend's gasp. "For now, I want to know who was there in the audience. Who did you see?"

"Good heavens, Eleanor. I saw just about everybody who was anybody. Do you want me to list them all?"

"Yes, please."

"Gracious, you don't want much."

Eleanor said nothing and started writing as Ann reeled off a list of names. Her friend had always had a phenomenal memory and a very good eye for spotting attendees at functions. Eleanor's own observation skills were pretty sharp, but in her own estimation they weren't a patch on Ann's.

"Hang on, I'm going to have to turn the page. All right, carry on."

"Haven't you had enough, yet? Now, where was I? Oh, yes, the Right Honourable Giles Frobisher and wife, the playwright Arthur Prince..."

Another twenty names were added to Eleanor's sheet of paper.

"There," Ann said, "that's as many as I can recall right off. Will it do you?"

"Marvellously! Thanks, Ann."

"I don't suppose you are going to tell me what you need to know all these names for..."

"Later. I've got to go."

"Wait! I know! You are investigating David Bristol's death. I knew it! Didn't I say you would?"

Eleanor heard the gurgle of laughter and smiled to herself. "Let's just say that I've received another commission. I'll see you tomorrow at Totters' place."

She replaced the receiver firmly, and carried her notebook to her chair by the fireside. Tracing a finger down the list of names, she nodded to herself a few times and began marking them with ticks, crosses, and question marks.

Then she let out a huge sigh. She might need to go back to the theatre and sweet talk the manager into supplying each person's seat or box number.

"Excuse me, my lady." Tilly walked in from the kitchen. "Would a cheese omelette be all right for your ladyship's lunch?"

"Indeed, Tilly, thank you. That will be perfect. As I have a new job, I shall celebrate by opening a bottle of red to go with it. The 1910 Pomerol, I think."

"Very good, my lady, I'll see to that. It won't take long."

Tilly darted back the way she had come and Eleanor continued to ponder the death of Sir David Bristol.

She made a number of notes, including one to speak to Danny Danvers again. He should be able to give her the low down on some of his boss's associates and whether there was any love lost between them.

Perhaps she could ask Totters about him, too. Now that he was a working journalist, he might have heard something about the owner of the Daily Banner, and be prepared to divulge it. Tomorrow night would be soon enough for that. Although it was a celebration, she should be able to get him to herself for a few minutes and ask his opinion of Bristol. For all she knew, he might have been a member of White's club, too.

She ate a solitary lunch — Tilly said she'd had a sandwich and was now busy rolling out pastry — but asked her maid to join her for coffee afterwards.

"You look troubled, my lady," Tilly said as she took a seat opposite her mistress at the fireside.

Eleanor had topped up her glass before leaving the table and now stared into the ruby depths of her wine and nodded.

"I am, Tilly old thing, I am. Something is going off and I don't understand it. That always troubles me. I also think that I have to call Major Armitage, and that troubles me, too."

On hearing the major's name Tilly sniffed, making Eleanor smile, for a single sniff of Tilly's could speak volumes, and mostly on the same theme.

Sniff — I wouldn't do that if I were you.

Sniff — You go ahead and do it, but don't say I didn't warn you.

Sniff — Of all the darn stupid things to do, but you're the mistress, I'm only the maid, and what do I know?

"Yes, I know what you think of him, but following this morning's interview I have information that he really ought to know about. I'm aware that I said I wouldn't get involved, but as a law-abiding citizen, and someone who holds this country dear, I simply cannot not tell him. I'm in a cleft stick, and it's largely one of my own making."

"You must do what you think best, my lady. Follow your conscience, like you always do."

"I know, Tilly." Eleanor sipped some wine and changed the subject. "So what did you think to our visitor?"

Tilly smiled. "Oh, very glamorous. In that black outfit she looked like a real grieving widow, didn't she?"

"Gosh yes."

"Of course, you have to remember she's an actress."

"Ah, you noticed that, did you?"

"Oh yes, as soon as I opened the door to her. If I may say so, my lady, although I was only the maid, she saw me as her audience and just slipped into the role she'd decided to play."

"That's very perspicacious of you, Tilly. I must say that I got that impression, too, but she seemed genuine enough in wanting to know who killed Bristol."

"So, you're going to take the case on, then?"

Eleanor wrinkled her nose. "Yes, I think so. She did offer me five hundred pounds."

"How much?" Tilly looked outraged.

"Actually, she told me to name my price, and that was just one of the figures she mentioned."

"Blimey! It must pay well to be an actress. Either that or she's got more money than sense."

Privately, Eleanor wondered if, as well as being his mistress, Deanna Dacre had received money from Bristol. For her to offer the sums she had, she must have had an income over and above what she was paid for acting.

"What do you know of Miss Dacre, Tilly? What have you read or heard about her?"

Tilly was an avid reader of cinema fan magazines, but as far as Eleanor knew, Deanna Dacre had not made the move away from the stage and her maid might not be such a follower if the actress had not appeared on the silver screen.

"Only the usual sort of thing, my lady, and most of that is made up, I reckon, just to get you to buy newspapers and magazines." The cynical Tilly shook her head at the goings-on of publishers. "She's supposed to be twenty-six years old and although the American film industry are keen to have her over there, she claims that she would prefer to stay in this country and remain on the stage. I'd love to see her act — on the stage, I mean. They do say she has immense talent."

"Oh, I can vouch for that, but I'm not so sure about her morals. She told me that Sir David Bristol had promised to put money into her latest play, only if she became his mistress."

"And she accepted?"

"Yes, she did."

This brought forth the anticipated sniff. Tilly wasn't prudish, but she had her own moral compass.

"Then she's no better than she ought to be," she remarked.

"Oh, I don't know." Eleanor rang a finger around the rim of her wine glass. "It may take two to have an affair, but he was the one to suggest it."

"She says. For all you know she seduced him because she was after his money."

Eleanor wondered if that were the case, and if it had backfired on Deanna Dacre. It hadn't stopped Bristol having other lovers, if there was any truth in the tale of Countess Vera Ivanova, nor had he been gentle with her, if the story of him assaulting Deanna were to be believed.

"Hmm. When Peter Armitage called here the other evening, he remarked that whoever had killed Bristol had done them a favour. Perhaps he's also done Deanna one."

"So, what do you intend to do, now?" Tilly poured herself a cup of coffee. She had made a pot for them both and, until now, waited for her mistress before broaching it. There was no point in letting it go cold and Eleanor still nursed her wine.

"I'm not sure. At some point I shall have to go back to the theatre. Ann Carstairs has given me a list of some of the people who were there and —"

"And me? What can I do?"

Eleanor glanced up at the clock on the mantelshelf. "You could go to the Viceroy, if you would, and take a note to Deanna Dacre that I shall give you. Then bring her reply back here."

"Yes, all right." Tilly brightened. She might not approve of the actress after what she'd just learned, but she was still a star to Tilly.

"While you're gone, I shall telephone Major Armitage, and then I may go and call at the offices of the Daily Banner. I want to gather as much gossip as I can about their erstwhile owner and that seems like a good place to start."

Chapter 14

With Tilly off on her errand, Eleanor picked up the telephone and gave the Major's number.

"I can't speak at the moment, my lady," he said, when they were connected. "Do you remember the cafe I took you to during the Eisenbach affair? Could you meet me there?"

"Yes, I think I should find it again. I'm going to the offices of the Daily Banner, so shall we say around four o'clock?"

Happy with this arrangement, Eleanor ended the conversation, called for the Lagonda to be brought around, then sped off to Fleet Street.

Here among the hustle and bustle associated with the home of Britain's national newspapers, and next to St Bride's church, she found her destination.

Entering the building felt like entering the lion's den, and heads turned as her elegant figure crossed the lobby and made for the reception desk. She heard more than one wolf-whistle which she ignored while smiling inwardly to herself. Her decision to dress to impress was paying off, even if only to the general workforce. Eleanor had bigger fish to catch.

She gave her name to the man at the desk, asked to speak to the editor, and after a short delay was shown up to his office on the top floor.

"What can I do for you, Lady Eleanor? Take a seat."

The grizzled man in his late fifties, wearing an open-necked shirt and braces, eyed her closely, then nodded to himself as if in approval of what he saw. Cuthbert Driscoll had worked in Fleet Street since he'd started as a runner at the age of eleven. In that time he had met and interviewed an awful lot of women, but none with such an air of cool assurance and self-possession as the attractive young woman who now stood before him.

He wasn't to know that Eleanor felt like a naughty schoolgirl in front of the headteacher.

"Thank you, Mr Driscoll, and thank you for sparing the time to see me." She waved a hand in an attempt to dispel some of the cigarette smoke that filled the room. "I'm a private enquiry agent, and have been asked to look into the murder of Sir David Bristol on behalf of Miss Deanna Dacre."

"Have you indeed!" Driscoll leaned back in his chair, hands clasped behind his head. "And what is it you think I can tell you? That I haven't already told the police, that is."

Eleanor smiled impishly at him. "Oh, I have no doubt that Chief Inspector Blount will get his man — or woman, should that prove to be the case — though the police are unlikely to discuss their findings with Miss Dacre."

"And *you* will?" He reached for a packet of cigarettes.

"Should I uncover anything, yes. I'll also inform the police in that case, too."

He leaned forward quickly. "What about this newspaper? If I tell you what you want to know, will you give us an exclusive interview on how you solved it?"

Eleanor hadn't expected that and took a moment to consider the proposition. As she'd told the Banner's reporter, she had absolutely no intention of having her name splashed across the paper's front page together with a photograph of her standing open-mouthed because the camera man had taken her by surprise. She shuddered at the mere thought of the notoriety that would bring her.

"Perhaps we can do a deal, Mr Driscoll."

"Oh, how so?"

"I am already in touch with your reporter, Mr Danvers. On the proviso that my name, and my photograph, appear nowhere in your paper, I will give him the full story, to go with his byline, on the completion of my investigation."

"Hmm." The editor puffed at his cigarette, sending grey clouds puthering upward, then slapped the desk. "Done. All right, your ladyship. I've got deadlines, so I'll give you ten minutes to ask whatever you like."

Eleanor nodded and spoke quickly, making the most of her opportunity.

"Did you know him well, sir?"

A sour look twisted the lined, tired face. "As well as I wanted to. He bought the paper approximately five years ago, and while I'll admit that he improved our failing fortunes, it came at a price."

"He used the Banner as a political mouthpiece, you mean?"

"I do indeed."

"Did he work from here?"

Driscoll shook his head. "He had a private office further along this floor, but hardly ever used it. For the most part, the day-to-day running of the place was left to me and my team of sub-editors, and the print and distribution managers."

While he was talking, Eleanor slipped her notebook and pen from her bag and began jotting things down.

"Bristol had a suite of offices on Bromwich Street, number 23, and ran his various business ventures from there. You'll find his secretary there, Miss Maud Haringay. She's an efficient woman, but I warn you, she bites." He gave an avuncular smile and Eleanor almost warmed to him. Almost, but not quite.

"I take it you know of his relationship with Miss Dacre."

It wasn't a question, more a statement of fact. Eleanor doubted that much got past the attention of the man on the other side of the desk.

"And I assume you were told to keep it out of the paper. Is that right?"

"Yes, of course, though we were allowed to sing her praises regarding her work on the stage, naturally enough." He scratched at his cheek with ink stained fingers. "Bristol once told me that if so much as a breath of scandal about either himself or Dacre appeared in the Banner, then he'd sack the lot of us. He would have done, too."

"He can't have been easy to work for."

"Oh, he was easy, he just wasn't pleasant. It's only two days since I wrote and printed his obituary, and I kept it to a mere biography — I had no sympathy, either with him or his politics, to turn it into a eulogy."

"Between you and me, Mr Driscoll, Deanna Dacre described him as shady. She thought his business practices suspect. Would you agree with that assessment?"

Driscoll let out a whistle, his grey bushy eyebrows rising. "I really couldn't say, your ladyship. I knew little of his other dealings. He seemed honest enough in his dealings with me and the Banner, but I didn't trust him an inch. It always struck me as odd that Bristol, a capitalist if ever I met one, should use the paper to promulgate Socialist dogma and push Socialist policies."

"Did he write his own editorials?" Eleanor wondered how much say the editor-in-chief had had in what appeared in the Banner.

"Yes. Oh, don't get me wrong, we are all working men on this newspaper, but some of the things we printed...well..." He shook his head, frowning.

"Did anyone here, any member of staff, have a grievance against Sir David? Mr Danvers said he'd had a row with him not that long since."

Driscoll laughed, the lines around his eyes deepening. "Yes, I heard about that. Danvers was in his cups, and he's an argumentative bugger at the best of times, begging your ladyship's pardon. Mind, he's a good reporter. I've no doubt he'll get his promotion soon." He gave Eleanor a shrewd glance. "I can see where you are going with this, my lady, but no one at the Banner, myself and Danvers included, had any reason to murder Bristol. You can take my word on that."

Could she? Eleanor wasn't so sure. Driscoll seemed mild mannered enough, for an editor, but she hadn't ruffled his feathers. There would be time for that if she could connect anyone at the Banner with a plausible motive for killing its owner. She got to her feet.

"Thank you for your time, Mr Driscoll," she said again. "I appreciate the help. May I come back if I think of anything else?"

The editor lit another cigarette and considered her request. "Aye, why not?" he said. "If nothing else, you brighten up the place."

Eleanor took this in the spirit it was intended, as a compliment, and left him to it.

She didn't however leave the building, or even the floor, but went in search of Sir David Bristol's office. The door was locked, but that presented no obstacle to someone who had been trained in lock-picking by none other than Peter Armitage.

The obstacle was provided by Eleanor's own conscience. She had given much thought to how far she would go in order to achieve her objectives and whether she was prepared to commit a crime in order to solve one. The answer to that had been 'yes', within reason and if the end justified the means.

With visions of newspaper headlines screaming, *Duke's daughter charged with breaking and entering*, Eleanor hung back. Hadn't Driscoll told her that

Bristol had offices elsewhere? So, the chances of there being anything of interest behind the locked door were minimal, and breaking in wasn't worth the risk.

With a sigh of relief mixed with disappointment she replaced the hairpin she had already taken from her hat, and walked back down the corridor to the stairs.

She chatted for a while to the reporters in the newsroom, though they largely reiterated what the editor had said, that Bristol was not a pleasant man to work for.

"Liked to claim he represented the working man, yet could barely pass the time of day with one."

"More interested in money, if you ask me."

"And that mistress of his."

"Aw, come on, Sid. Who wouldn't be interested in the divine Dacre, eh? Bit of all right, she is."

Eleanor thanked them and went back to the car. Bristol sounded such a horrid man, she was beginning to wish she'd refused the job Deanna Dacre had pushed upon her.

Chapter 15

Thinking that her journey to Fleet Street had been largely a waste of time, Eleanor drove away and considered what approach she should take with Bristol's secretary, Miss Haringay.

She had been happy to name her client to Driscoll, whom she took to be a man of the world, but any mention of Deanna Dacre might not go down so well at her next port of call.

Bromwich Street lay in an area of London that was unfamiliar to Eleanor. She drove around the surrounding streets, acquainting herself with the area for some little time before she parked and walked to the entrance of what had once been an elegant Georgian townhouse, similar to the Bakewells' own.

In the open plan lobby, an exceedingly glamorous receptionist possessed of a large bosom flashed Eleanor a toothy smile and demanded to know how she could help. The smile beat a fast retreat at the mention of Miss Haringay's name, however, and she took Eleanor's card as gingerly as if it were on fire, and disappeared with it through a side door.

Left to her own devices, Eleanor stared around at the opulent surroundings, not much changed since the days when Number 23 had been a private residence. A pair of fine oil paintings hung on one wall, portraits of previous owners, perhaps, and she strode across for a closer look.

The paintings were dark with age and so in need of cleaning it was impossible to see who had painted them. Maybe Totters with his degree in Fine Art would have been able to identify and tell her more about the artist, but Eleanor's attention was in the detail of the clothing which was lavishly embroidered, each stitch clear and precise upon the canvas even under the murk and grime.

She stared so intently that she almost missed the conversation taking place some distance behind her. The voices of a man and a woman were low, but distinct.

"The shoulder isn't important now. I know it's Thursday."

"You're sure of that?"

"Quite sure. Nine o'clock. Don't be late."

"I am never late," came the waspish reply.

The man's voice was unmistakeable, but the woman's voice, although distinctive, was unknown. Eleanor did not turn around. She stepped closer to the wall and lowered her head to peer at the painting.

A cold draft on her ankles announced the opening of the front door and she shifted her position slightly, careful to keep her back to the opening and the two people on the step.

"Have no fear." The man's voice was confident. "We shan't fail."

The second voice was muted in reply before the door closed.

Eleanor went over the conversation, fixing every word in her mind. She would report it to Armitage later.

"Lady Eleanor Bakewell?"

A hand fell on her arm. Eleanor looked down at it. "Yes?"

"I'm Miss Haringay. You wished to see me?"

The waspish voice went with a waspish face. Small, grey haired, and wearing a pair of wire-framed spectacles on her sharp bony nose, Sir David Bristol's secretary had clearly been chosen for her competence, not her looks.

"Yes, Miss Haringay. I am a private enquiry agent and I wondered if you could spare me a few minutes please, regarding the death of Sir David Bristol."

The secretary's thin-lipped mouth tightened, giving the impression of having just sucked a lemon. Impossible to avoid the assumption that Miss Haringay made a habit of such an activity, because she enjoyed it.

"Very well, you had better come through to my office."

She led the way to the door that the receptionist, who was now back at the desk and writing assiduously, had previously entered. The room appeared little bigger than a cubicle, an effect mainly due to the amount of space occupied by filing cabinets.

A large map of the world covered the wall behind the desk in the centre of the room which itself was covered with a map and a multitude of papers. Miss

Haringay scooped everything into a drawer before picking up the telephone and telling the switchboard operator that she was not to be disturbed.

"Now then, your ladyship, would you tell me what concern the passing of Sir David is of yours?"

"I have been retained by a client to look into the circumstances of his murder and —"

"What client?" The thin mouth snapped.

"I'm afraid I am not at liberty to say. I'm sure you are familiar with the concept of client confidentiality."

"Indeed." She tilted her head to one side, the small dark eyes taking in every aspect of Eleanor's appearance. She picked up her visitor's business card. "If I may say so, a private enquiry agent seems an unlikely role for a lady."

Eleanor didn't miss the implication of the words.

"My father, the Duke of Bakewell would no doubt agree with you. I will, however, admit to an interest of my own in Sir David's tragic death. I was at the Viceroy theatre that evening, and found his body."

"Dear me." The eyes behind the spectacles flickered. "Did you see who shot him?"

Eleanor shook her head. "Sadly not."

"Well, I know nothing about it, so why come to me?"

"Because I didn't know the man, and you did. What line of business was he in?"

A shrug from the other side of the desk. "Sir David had many interests. As well as owning the Daily Banner he had business dealings around the world."

"So I see," Eleanor said. She stood up and crossed to the map, noting the coloured pins with which it was studded. "Paris, Rome, Berlin. Did he travel to all these places?"

Miss Haringay had not moved from her desk. "Sometimes. He also owned several import and export companies."

"And what did they deal in?" Eleanor returned to her seat, noting the secretary's furious glare.

"Various commodities."

There was more chance of getting blood out of a stone than information out of Maud Haringay. While acknowledging that this would be an essential and necessary attribute when dealing with sensitive business matters, it did not help Eleanor in her task.

"Did Sir David have any enemies, anyone that he might have wronged in business, perhaps?"

"Certainly not. He was a most ethical man. In the cut and thrust of the business community it is sometimes an advantage to do your opponent down. Sir David never would."

Eleanor doubted this. Driscoll had said that Bristol was not a pleasant man to work for, and Deanna would not have called her lover shady had he been as ethical and honest as his secretary was trying to make out.

She might have been in love with him, of course, but that was one question Eleanor wasn't prepared to ask.

"Had you worked for him long, Miss Haringay?"

"Nigh on thirty years."

"And who will take over now that he is gone?"

"I couldn't say. I am sure he made provisions for the respective companies and that will be in his will, which hasn't been read as yet. Personally, I shall retire. Sir David always said that he would leave me well provided for, and I have my eye on a little cottage in the village of Haversham. I shall read, and devise crossword puzzles."

This was quite a speech for the taciturn Miss Haringay, and the adroit change of subject had not escaped Eleanor's notice.

"Are you a devotee of crosswords?" she asked.

"Yes, I have been since I did the first one in Pearson's magazine a year or so back. They are greatly to be recommended for improving one's vocabulary and mental acuity, in my estimation."

Miss Haringay's mind was sharp enough. Eleanor wondered what she was missing, and whether, like a conjuror, the secretary was distracting her attention away from what really mattered — whatever that might be.

"And the theatre? Were you perhaps there that evening?"

Miss Haringay's gaze fell to her desk. "No. I have no interest in drama."

Eleanor nodded. "We were talking about enemies," she said. "Sir David had probably made political enemies with his espousal of the Labour party. Do you —"

"Tsk tsk." Miss Haringay waved a finger at Eleanor. "A man's politics are his own, as the saying has it. Of course, I don't expect a lady to know anything of business, but, as Sir David often said, politics sells papers. You make the mistake, as a lot of people did, of assuming that what appeared in the Daily Banner was an accurate reflection of the proprietor's own beliefs."

"Were they not?"

The secretary's words might explain a lot. Eleanor had found it hard to reconcile Bristol's wealth and his style of living — yachts in the South of France, private boxes at the theatre — with his supposed socialist tendencies. The two did not fit well together and Eleanor was fast beginning to think him a hypocrite. Miss Haringay, though she might not know it, so keen did she seem to point out her employer's great business acumen, had confirmed this.

"I doubt it, though it was not a subject we discussed."

Eleanor shook her head, unsure of how, or even whether, to continue. The task Deanna Dacre had given her seemed hopeless.

"Have you any idea who might have killed Sir David, Miss Haringay?"

"None whatsoever, and I told the policeman from Scotland Yard the same. His death is a sad loss to everyone here and a total mystery."

A sad loss? Yet Miss Haringay appeared dry-eyed. Had she even shed a tear for her employer? Eleanor thought it doubtful.

There were many more questions she wanted to ask, but the secretary had decided that the time she had available for private detectives was at an end and rose to her feet.

"I am sorry that I am unable to help you further, Lady Eleanor. No doubt the police will bring the miscreant to justice before too long."

She gave Eleanor a tight-lipped condescending smile on her way to open the office door. If it was meant to crush her spirits it had completely the opposite effect, strengthening Eleanor's resolve and stiffening her spine. She, too, rose in one graceful and fluid movement.

"Thank you for your time, Miss Haringay. It has been most instructive." She smiled down at the now scowling secretary as she sailed past. "I'll show myself out. Good afternoon."

However, she did not feel so sanguine as she drove away from Bromwich Street in search of the cafe and her rendezvous with Major Armitage.

"If that secretary is mourning her boss, then I'm the Queen of Sheba," she said, slapping the Lagonda's leather-bound steering wheel with a gloved hand. "I'll swear she lied about not being at the Viceroy that evening, just as I'm sure she knows something about Bristol's death. It seems, though, that I'm going to have as much success in this case as I did in finding Barbara Lancashire's pearls. Precisely zero."

Chapter 16

Major Armitage was waiting for her, already seated at a table at the rear of the small cafe when Eleanor arrived. She apologised for her lateness and took the seat opposite as he called the waitress over.

"Are you all right," he asked, when he'd placed their order. "You look slightly flustered."

"Only slightly?" Eleanor removed her hat and placed it on one of the empty chairs. "It's only that I've been rushing. I didn't want to keep you waiting, but I was having my ears bitten off."

"Really?" He tilted his head first to the right, then the left. "Your ears look perfectly fine to me."

He gave her the sort of warm, tender smile that made her go limp in all the wrong places and, out of sight underneath the table, she dug her fingernails into her palms. She wasn't going to fall for his soft-soap. No matter how attractive she found him, no matter the way her heart raced when he was near, Peter Armitage was a dark and dangerous man, and she would do well to remember that.

"If you don't behave," she said, in mock severity, "then I shan't tell you why I called and asked to meet you."

"You mean it wasn't for the thrill of my scintillating conversation, my rib-tickling jokes, and my boyish good looks? How dashed disappointing."

Eleanor gaped at him. This light-hearted, jovial and jesting major was an unimagined creature. Apart from those few hours of shared tenderness a long time ago, the Peter Armitage she knew was a dour and serious man. It came as something of a shock to realise she didn't know him at all.

She glanced down, covering her smile. "Sadly no, but I do have an awful lot to tell you, Major."

He was instantly serious. "All right, let's have it."

She began by telling him of the commission from Deanna Dacre and followed that with an account of her visits to the Banner and Bristol's office in Bromwich Street.

As usual he listened attentively and without interruption, sipping his tea, and stroking the small scar on his chin from time to time.

"Conclusion?" He rapped when she had finished.

Eleanor grinned. "That Bristol was not a nice man. A violent bully and a hypocrite. I'm glad I didn't know him. I don't know if that is any help to you, or to me either. I haven't had time yet to sit and think it over, but there is one thing that may interest you. Something I overheard at Bromwich Street while I waited for Miss Haringay."

"Which was?"

Her report was almost as brief as the conversation had been, but Armitage's eyes lit up when she told him who the secretary had been talking to.

"Yes, you're right. That is interesting. We had been wondering about him. Any idea what they were talking about? Thursdays and shoulders? Sounds like it could have been in code."

"Sorry, Major. No idea at all. I made sure that I kept my back to them — I didn't want to be recognised, nor appear to be eavesdropping — but that meant I couldn't see any facial expressions that might have helped. It's something else I have to mull over when I have time."

"Time? We haven't got time. That meeting —"

"I haven't forgotten." She drummed her fingers on the table. "Is Chief Inspector Blount aware of this meeting you're so worried about?"

Armitage scowled. "Only peripherally. National security and all that. Why do you ask?"

"Because he can ask the questions that I can't." She wrinkled her nose at her own perceived failings, and ground her teeth in frustration. "And he can insist on answers. I can't ask people if they killed someone, or where they were at the time someone was killed. They'd laugh in my face and tell me to mind my own business if I did. But Blount can."

"So? Your 'softly, softly, catchee monkey' approach worked wonders last time."

"Yes, but I wasn't under a deadline then. I should never have listened to Ann."

"Ann?"

"Lady Ann Carstairs. It was her suggestion that I set myself up as a private enquiry agent, and I'm flaming useless at it."

She made a fist and would have thumped the table with it, had his hand not shot out and closed over it.

"Gently, my lady." He gave a quick glance over her shoulder, but the cafe was quiet at this hour. There were no tables behind theirs and Eleanor realised he had chosen their seats with his customary care.

"I'm sorry, Peter. The frustration is getting the better of me."

"Then I'm sorry to have put so much extra pressure on you." He smiled and shook his head. "It's your own fault."

"Oh? How?"

"You're too good an operative."

"Was." She hissed the word. "How often do I have to keep telling you?" She couldn't decide whether to put her head in her hands and sob, or to slap him, and it took all of her restraint to do neither of those things.

He held up a hand. "I know, and I'm sorry to keep harping on about it, but if you could see some of the specimens I have to work with, then you'd realise my own frustration." He waved an airy hand as if dismissing the subject. "So, what are you going to do now?"

Eleanor tilted her head and thought about it. "I'm going home and I shall soak the stress of the day away with a warm bath and then, if I haven't fallen asleep, I'm going to an engagement party."

"Well, I hope you have an enjoyable evening. You will —"

"Keep my ear to the ground, yes."

"No," he said, sober faced. "Don't do that, or folks will wonder why you're impersonating a bloodhound with an itchy face, scratching it on the carpet."

It took a moment to realise that he was joking again, and she gave a polite laugh. "My father always likened me to a poodle when I was younger because of my curly hair. I'll have to tell him about the bloodhound. He'll appreciate that."

"Seriously, see what you can find out, will you."

"What about you? Are you going to follow up on Miss Haringay and that rather odd conversation?"

"Oh, yes. That could be our best lead yet. She sounds the type to have been devoted to Bristol, and was probably as involved in his covert activities as much as she was in his business dealings. Perhaps she's trying to complete the job he started."

Eleanor sipped at her tea, replaced the cup in her saucer, and shook her head. Men could be so blind sometimes. It surprised her that Armitage had not seen the alternative to his theory, but then, he hadn't seen the martinet behind the desk.

"You don't agree?" he asked.

"You're probably right, and I'm sure she was lying about not being at the Viceroy that night, but have you considered that Miss Haringay herself may be the leader of the gang? She'd be safely hidden behind Bristol's coat tails, as it were, and there's plenty of precedence for a female ringleader, though there's very little that's feminine about the redoubtable Miss Haringay."

Armitage pursed his lips, eyebrows rising. "Yes, I suppose that might be the case."

"Well, then, can't you round them up, throw them in the Tower, and interrogate them? Or, better yet, ask Mr MacDonald and Mr Doumergue to delay their meeting until you've got the assassin under lock and key?"

"It doesn't work like that, you know. This is a free country and, at the moment, I have no grounds for arresting anyone. As for the Prime Minister and his guest...I rather think they'd give short shrift to any suggestion that a coven of spies and assassins dictated their movements." He let out a long sigh. "My job would be so much easier if politicians and royalty would take the Intelligence Services' worries seriously, and do what they were told."

Eleanor reached for her hat and repositioned it on her blonde head. "I'm sorry, but I must go. I'll make time to think things over before I go to Tommy Totteridge's party. I don't suppose that I shall learn anything relative to this affair tonight, but I will keep my eyes and ears open."

He reached across and took her hand. "Please call me tomorrow if you uncover anything that you think will help. No matter how small."

"Of course."

Perturbed and exasperated, Eleanor drove home and put herself in Tilly's hands.

She relaxed in rose scented bath water and let her thoughts drift. Refusing to be infected by the Major's sense of urgency, she moved her limbs and let the lapping water carry her cares away.

Once she was out of the bath and dried, Tilly rubbed scented lotion into her mistress's legs and back, massaging Eleanor's shoulders and 'getting the knots out' as she put it.

When Eleanor was finished being pampered, she dressed and sat at the dressing table while Tilly brushed her hair and added a jewelled clasp.

"There, my lady. You'll be the belle of the ball."

Eleanor eyed her reflection sourly. "Hardly, Tilly, but thank you. I must admit, I feel that I've had such a dashed awful day, that if tonight's shindig wasn't in honour of dear old Totters and his lady, I'd think twice about going and settle for a night at home."

"Nonsense, my lady. You go and enjoy yourself. If you've had as bad a day as you say, then you deserve it."

"Do I? I seem to have achieved nothing."

Tilly leaned back against the wardrobe and crossed her arms over her chest. "Not necessarily. You've barely had chance to think about things, yet. Go and have a good time then, after a night's rest, you may start to see things a little clearer and make sense of them."

Eleanor stood up and gave her maid a hug. "What would I do without you?"

"You'd do well enough. Now, off you go, and please offer my congratulations to Mr Totteridge and Miss Westlake."

"Of course."

"And stay out of trouble."

"When do I ever get into trouble?"

Tilly sniffed.

Chapter 17

Laughter and the chink of glasses greeted Eleanor on her arrival at Totters' flat. His man let her in and relieved her of her coat. "The drinks are in the kitchen, my lady."

He might have added that the drunks were in the living room by the sounds of revelry Eleanor could hear. She went on through to greet her hosts and the twenty or so other guests before making for the kitchen.

"Hello, darling. You look like you could use one of these." Lady Ann sat on the table and waved a cocktail glass at Eleanor. "It's Totters' own recipe. Hic! Who knew the man had such talents? I'd have snaffled him myself if I'd realised. Cheers!"

"What's in it?" Eleanor found a clean glass and took the cocktail shaker from Ann's outstretched hand.

"Well, there's vodka for a start, and I think he said something about Galliano and something else, but I can't remember. Anyway, it's delish! Cheers!"

Eleanor poured a small amount into her glass, smelling the contents before she tried a sip. Lady Ann was not as drunk as she pretended to be, but Eleanor intended to keep a clear head.

"Very nice. How many have you had?"

"This is only my second. I awarded it to myself for organising this bash, which as you can hear is going very well." She waved a hand in the direction of the main room, crossed one silk-stockinged leg over the other and examined her friend critically. "What's up, Eleanor? You've taken the merest sip and are now staring moodily at it, as if it were ditch water."

Eleanor looked up and smiled. "Was I? I'm sorry. I've been out all day working on the Bristol case and I'm still puzzling over it."

"Cheer up, oh, intrepid sleuth." Ann grinned. "Tell me what Deanna Dacre was really like. What did she wear?"

For the next few minutes, Eleanor satisfied her friend's request and laughed when she commented that, "you'd have expected, given the money she must have, that the Divine Deanna would have worn something better than widow's weeds. Huh!"

"Ah, but she was playing the role, I think. I tell you, she didn't stop being an actress from the moment she knocked on my door to the moment she left. It was quite a performance."

"Cynic." Ann dropped down from the table. "Come on, let's join the others. I've brought some records over for Totters' gramophone and it's about time we put them on and danced."

Arm in arm they joined the rest of the gathering.

"There you are, Lady Eleanor." Sophie walked towards them. "I was just coming to look for you. Come and join us, we need a detective."

"Whatever for?" Eleanor looked around the sea of faces, all strangely quiet, and wondered what was happening? "Is this a joke? Are you playing parlour games?"

"Not on your life, Eleanor." Totters grinned at her from the depths of an armchair. "This is deadly serious. Tell her, Ariadne."

Eleanor glanced at the Honourable Ariadne Beresford, a small whey-faced creature with protuberant eyes and, it was rumoured, a remarkable capacity for drink.

"Well, why not?" She shrugged. "I don't suppose it will do any harm. I was just telling everyone that we had a burglary two nights ago and mother's emerald necklace was stolen."

"There's a lot of it going off right now." This came from a tall man who leaned one arm against the mantelpiece. "I hear that opera singer woman that's in town, Scarletti I think her name is, lost a diamond tiara on Monday."

In the general hubbub Ann leaned towards Eleanor. "It seems your case isn't the only one. There's definitely a clever jewel thief behind all this."

Eleanor wrinkled her nose. Was Barbara Lancashire's pearl necklace down to the same thief, or had someone else taken advantage of the current spate of thefts?

Tommy stilled the noise with a hand. "What do you make of it, Eleanor, old thing? Perhaps Ariadne ought to ask her mother to hire you."

"I don't know that I make anything of it, unless...Ariadne, did your mother have guests that evening?"

"Yes, as a matter of fact she did."

"And the diva gave a recital in her suite when the tiara disappeared," the man at the fireplace chimed in.

"Ah ha! Eleanor, you're on to something." Totters looked around at the gathering. "Didn't I tell you she was marvellous?"

"Stop it, Tommy," Eleanor protested, though she was laughing. "Ariadne, I'm looking into another instance of stolen jewels at the moment."

Strictly speaking, that was no longer true now that Barbara had dispensed with her services, but that in itself was mystery enough for an intrigued Eleanor to want to get to the bottom of it.

Ariadne nodded. "Oh, yes?"

"Do you think your mother might supply me with a list of her guests that evening?"

"Good Lord." Totters sat upright. "You think it's a guest who's stealing and not a burglar? What dashed bad form, what!"

"No, Tommy, I don't say that, and I'm not accusing anyone, but it might be as well to check, don't you think? To see if there's a pattern to these thefts."

A murmur of assent ran around the room.

"All right. I'll ask mother," Ariadne said.

Eleanor took a business card from her bag and passed it over. "Thanks. I assure you, I'll be discreet. Like I said, I doubt whoever is responsible is anyone you know or have invited into your home, but it would be as well to remove all doubt."

"You'd better make sure you lock up your valuables, Sophie, old girl," someone called.

"Nah." Sophie Westlake shook her sleek head and waved a hand on which a diamond ring flashed. "I trust all of you lot, and the only valuable I've got and care about is Tommy." She dropped a kiss on the top of his head, causing raucous laughter in some quarters, and plenty of oohs and aahs in others.

"Phew," Ann muttered. "That was close. You almost single-handedly put paid to everybody's social life. Just think, no more parties, soirées, or friendly get-togethers, all courtesy of Lady Eleanor Bakewell."

"Don't." Eleanor shook her head and buried her nose in her glass.

"That would have been my livelihood straight out of the window."

Ann could be remorseless when she put her mind to it. Eleanor hoped she was only joking, but what if she wasn't?

With a sigh, Eleanor wandered back into the kitchen in search of a refill to drown her sorrows. The cocktail shaker was empty, but an array of bottles on a shelf next to the larder caught her eye. She was just debating whether it was the done thing to help oneself when Sophie came in.

"Are you all right?" she asked. "Only you look a little worried. Is that because the shaker is empty or due to something else?"

Eleanor laughed. "Oh, the shaker, definitely."

Sophie was not so easily deceived. "Look, I know tonight is supposed to be a happy occasion, but that doesn't mean that everyone has to pretend to be happy if they're not. If you've got something on your mind that's bothering you, then spit it out. Maybe I can help. I can at least lend you a sympathetic ear."

"Thanks, Sophie, and I am happy for you and Totters. Have you set a wedding date?"

"Yes." Sophie walked past her and took down a selection of the bottles which she proceeded to pour into the shaker. "I'm going to be a June bride. Saturday the 14th of June, at St Martin-in-the-Fields. You'll get an invite, of course."

"Oh, that's wonderful! I shall be there."

Eleanor knew the beautiful church on the corner of Trafalgar Square and thought it a perfect venue for her friends.

"What about you?"

"What about me?"

Sophie gave the metal cylinder a vigorous shake and poured some of the concoction it contained into her own and Eleanor's glass.

"When are you going to find a man and settle down?"

"Oh, I shan't get married." Eleanor took a sip from her glass, and coughed. "Stap me!"

Sophie slapped her on the back. "That'll put hairs on your chest."

Eleanor got her breath back and laughed. "I'd rather they didn't. No one will want to marry me if I have a hairy chest. I shall stay an old maid, making the rounds of my friends, expecting to be fed, watered, and accommodated for days at a time, and they'll groan whenever they hear I'm at the door."

"Nonsense. You're a clever woman, you'll find yourself a man someday."

Eleanor smiled but made no answer. She wanted different things out of life. To her, getting married was not the whole point of existence that it appeared to be to Sophie. There had to be more in life than that.

Totters put on a gramophone record and the party became even livelier and noisier. Eleanor sat and nursed her drink and went home as soon as it was decent to do so.

"I don't fit in, Tilly," she told her maid as she got ready for bed. "There has to be more to life than parties and husbands, yet I'm a duke's daughter, expected to conform. To marry someone equal to my rank and breed more little future earls or countesses, lords and ladies. I don't want that, but I don't know what I do want."

Tilly hung up her mistress's dress and returned to rub Eleanor's shoulders.

"Yes, the war changed us, didn't it?"

"It doesn't appear to have changed anyone else." Eleanor sighed. "It's just me. Ann's got a job, and that keeps her happy, but it's still just parties. What is she going to do when the partying has to stop? Everyone else is marrying, settling down, and I feel so out of it. Oh, don't get me wrong, I'm very happy for them — especially Totters and Sophie — but I have nothing. I'm just a looker-on, a spectre at the feast."

"Then perhaps it is about time you found a man yourself, my lady."

"Don't you start." Eleanor grinned and threw a pillow at her maid.

"And you do have a job, remember. Private enquiry agent. Go to bed and perhaps in the morning you'll see your way clear to solving Sir David Bristol's murder. You're just feeling low because you don't appear to be making any progress on the case."

"You're probably right. Thank you, Tilly. Goodnight."

But as she lay in the darkness, going over the events of a long day in her mind, both sleep and a solution to the murder proved elusive. Someone had said something that she now thought important, though at the time it had passed her by.

She turned over, listening to the sound of rain against the window. The face of the Banner's editor flashed into her mind, swiftly followed by the prim features of Miss Haringay, and then that of the handsome, stern Major Armitage. She let his face linger, and called his words to mind.

"You're too good an operative."

Too good.

Too good.

She fell asleep with a smile on her face.

Chapter 18

Eleanor, nursing a bad head, remained silent during breakfast the next morning. She had drunk two cups of coffee before she trusted herself to speak, and then it was only to renounce drink.

"I shall never have cocktails again."

"Oh, I'm sure you will, my lady." Tilly's reply came in far too loud a voice for Eleanor's liking.

"Well, not one made by Sophie Westlake. That girl should be banned from being within half a mile of a cocktail shaker, let alone using one."

She refused Tilly's offer of bacon and eggs with a groan, but two slices of toast left Eleanor feeling much better, and at least able to face the day.

"How did you get on with Miss Dacre?" Eleanor asked as the two of them sat in the drawing room later.

"She was charming and even gave me a signed photograph of herself. I've never been backstage at a theatre before. I found it fascinating."

"And the answer to my note?"

"Ah, yes. Sir David knew the Lancashires, and Sir Oswald Brain. She didn't recognise the name of Hope-Weedon, so doesn't know if Sir David knew him or not."

Eleanor gave this a moment's thought. "Hmm, she's unlikely to forget Hope-Weedon. He's too attractive to be missed. All right, Tilly, thanks."

It had been a long shot that Armitage's suspects would be involved with Bristol, let alone have reason to murder him, but it had been worth asking the question of Deanna Dacre.

"What about you, my lady? Have you worked out why Lady Lancashire said she no longer needed you to look for her pearls? She must have been pleased if they hadn't been stolen after all."

"Oh, she was, and yet..." Eleanor paused. "Hang on to that thought, Tilly. You've got something there."

She pulled her legs up, heels resting on the seat, and wrapped her arms around her knees. Tilly sniffed.

"Yes," Eleanor said, after a moment's cogitation. "Yes, she was pleased, but it was a smug pleased, not the genuine pleasure you would get from finding an item you thought lost or stolen. I can't describe it, other than to say that it felt wrong somehow. And there was a sense of relief, too."

"Relief at not having to pay you, you mean?"

"No...o, I don't think that was it." A vision of Barbara Lancashire staring forlornly at her chequebook floated into Eleanor's mind. "Although it might have been, perhaps, if I hadn't been so quick to waive my fee...

"We can forget about the story of the pearls having been sent for cleaning. That was just poppycock, all my eye and Betty Martin, and it didn't ring true at all."

"So, what happened for Lady Lancashire to change her mind so rapidly? Why did she call you in one day, because the pearls had been stolen, and then tell you not to bother a day or so after?"

"Ah, Tilly. There's the rub."

Tilly's face acquired a sour look at the vagaries of those members of the gentry who didn't know their own mind. "It makes no sense."

"Doesn't it, though, Tilly? I think it might, you know." Eleanor unwound herself from the balled position she'd adopted, and stretched her legs. "Have you still got the newspaper with the report of Sir David Bristol's murder?"

"I think so. I kept it, seeing as you might want to look at it again, otherwise I'd have used it for kindling."

"Be a lamb and go and get it for me, then, will you?"

As her maid departed to the scullery, Eleanor considered the audacious idea that had come to mind following Tilly's questions.

"There you are." Tilly brought in a copy of the Times. "It's clean, if a bit crumpled. Do you want me to iron it?"

Eleanor laughed. "No, silly. It will be fine as it is, thank you."

She took the newspaper from her maid, and put it on the floor at her feet. The murder had made the front page and a grainy photograph of the sombre faced owner of the Daily Banner stared back at her as she bent over it.

"Have you solved it then?"

Eleanor glanced up. "I don't know, old girl, but I have had a preposterous idea just present itself. Sit down and tell me what you think, will you?"

"Yes, my lady." Tilly sat down again, perched on the edge of the settee.

Her mistress finished reading a paragraph, sat back, and lit a cigarette. "The thing that struck me the most when I first went to interview Lady Lancashire was not the account of the burglary, which even then I found somewhat spurious, but her insistence that she needed the pearls back. Needed them back, not wanted, you'll note. I thought then that it was an odd way to phrase it."

"Perhaps she needed them back for a specific reason, then?" Tilly pulled at her lower lip.

"Exactly!"

"And then something happened that meant she no longer needed them after all."

"Yes, that's my take on it, too. The preposterous idea is that Barbara Lancashire no longer needed her pearl necklace...because Sir David Bristol was dead."

"Eh?"

Eleanor puffed at her cigarette and grinned at Tilly. "Yes, I said it was preposterous, but what if?"

Tilly sniffed. "You'll forgive me saying so, my lady, but there's preposterous and there's downright daft."

"Oh, I'll grant you that it seems that way at the moment." Eleanor threw the remains of her cigarette into the fire. "That's because I'm lacking a motive."

"What for? If Lady Lancashire needed her pearls to give to Sir David, and didn't once he was dead, then why were you no longer needed? She still didn't have her necklace."

"Hmm. Also true. I hadn't thought of that. Oh, heavens what a muddle."

Excusing herself as she had things to do in the kitchen, Tilly went out, leaving her mistress to continue mulling things over by the fire.

Unable to resolve things by herself, she picked up the phone and asked to be put through to the Daily Banner.

Danny Danvers was in the newsroom and more than happy to speak to her.

"Got anything for me, your ladyship? It's dreadfully quiet around here at the moment. More like a morgue than a newsroom."

"Yes, I might have. I'd also like to pick your brains."

A deep chuckle echoed down the wire. "Are you sure it's just my brain you're after? I've better features than that, you know."

Eleanor laughed. "Quite sure, though thank you for the offer."

"Then, how about I take you for dinner tonight? I'll book a table and meet you outside *Rules* in Covent Garden at eight-thirty."

"*Rules*, eh? Can you afford it?"

The establishment laid claim to being the oldest restaurant in London, and also one of the most expensive. It was said that Edward VII and his mistress Lily Langtry had dined there in a private room. Eleanor hoped that Danvers intended eating in the main area; she didn't much fancy being closeted with him.

"Well," he said, "if you're not going to pay for me, then I suppose I'll have to."

"Oh, I'm an expensive lady to squire around the fleshpots of London, Mr Danvers."

"Thanks for the warning." He laughed. "I'll see you at eight-thirty."

Eleanor replaced the receiver with a smile. Had he been flirting with her? Or she with him? No matter, she enjoyed the easy banter with the charming reporter and looked forward to an evening in his company.

Promptly at half past eight Eleanor's taxi turned into Maiden Lane and dropped her off outside the restaurant.

Danvers stepped out from under its red and gold awning and put a hand under her elbow.

"Good evening, my lady. You obviously agree with the axiom that punctuality is the politeness of kings."

She smiled. "Of course, though I try not to get that far above myself."

Heads turned as Eleanor and her escort were shown to their table. Her long, sweeping dress was cut low at back and front. Tilly had remarked that the only thing holding it up was gravity, but admitted her mistress looked stunning in the peacock blue creation.

Among those heads, Eleanor noted that of Gerald Hope-Weedon and, at a table further on, Major Peter Armitage. She nodded and smiled to the former, who got to his feet and sketched a small bow, but the latter she ignored after catching the brief shake of his head.

"Now then, my lady," Danvers began after they'd perused the menu and placed their order with an attentive waiter. "This is a rare pleasure for a lowly newsman like myself. So, what have you got for me?"

"That depends. Have you heard anything more about Bristol's murder?"

He shook his head. "No, it's all gone rather quiet on that score. I keep sniffing around, but can't find much, and I doubt, given their silence, that the police have either. What about you?"

Eleanor wrinkled her nose. "Would you say he was capable of blackmail?"

"Jehoshaphat!" His eyebrows rose. "Well, yes, I would, but then as you've gathered, I didn't care for the man and wouldn't have put anything past him. Are we talking blackmail for business or pleasure purposes, here?"

She smiled at his turn of phrase, considering it very apt as well as biting. "Both. Certainly as a means to an end."

"What sort of an end?"

"A political one."

The arrival of a bottle of wine put paid to any further conversation for a while. Eleanor, who had telephoned the restaurant herself and ordered it in time for it to be opened and decanted, noted Danvers' glance of alarm and hurried to reassure him.

"I hope you don't mind," she said. "It's a terrible cheek on my part, but I wanted to make some contribution to the evening. After all, I called you."

"Ah, but it was I who asked you out."

The wine waiter, perhaps suspecting that a lovers' tiff lay in the offing, suavely intervened. "An excellent choice, if I may say so, my lady."

A few moments later, Danvers agreed with him. "Please feel free to order for me again, my lady. I've tasted nothing like that since I was in Paris on Armistice Day and the restaurateur insisted on opening his cellar. Ah, happy days."

The meal arrived a short while later and perfectly complemented the wine — and vice versa, as Danvers put it.

"Danny," Eleanor said, as they were about to tuck in, "what do you know about the chap at the table behind me and to your right? The one with a red rose in his lapel."

Danvers eyes never shifted from her face. "He's known as GHW in newspaper jargon. The man of the moment, a man going places. He's a little too sparkly clean for my taste." He grinned. "I'm an old cynic who trusts no one. Why do you want to know?"

Eleanor picked up her wine glass. "You know nothing to his detriment, then?"

"Can't say that I do." His brow furrowed. "You're being very intriguing this evening."

"I did say I wanted to pick your brains."

"So you did. I hope you'll leave some for me. They're quite useful, I'm told, especially in my line of work."

Eleanor laughed. "Don't worry, I shall. I hear he's keen to become Foreign Secretary. So what then do you make of the head of that department, Sir Robert Lancashire?"

"Oh, he's all right. He's a competent fellow, inclined to keep himself to himself, and hide behind his wife, but generally speaking he's well liked, even respected."

"Do you know his wife?"

"I have met her, but I wouldn't go so far as to say I know her." He gave a sly grin. "Unlike present company, she's not my type."

Determined to give him no encouragement, Eleanor ignored the playful banter. "I'd also like you to take me gambling later, in whichever is the best place in town."

Danvers had been about to take a sip of wine and put the glass down.

"On your money, I hope. I don't earn enough to throw it away on the spin of a wheel or the turn of a card. Besides, gambling is rather frowned upon you know, and I'd hate to get arrested."

"Yes, that's understood. I'm not trying to have you locked up or fleece you. Shall we call it research?" She smiled archly. "I'll explain it all when we are somewhere more private. Somewhere we are unlikely to be overheard."

As soon as she'd said it, Eleanor thought of Major Armitage and cast a glance in his direction. She wondered who he was with, and ignored the feeling of relief that he appeared to have no female companion of his own, for he sat with an older couple who had their backs to her. Perhaps they were his parents, or maybe his boss and his wife.

Why was he there? She remembered his shake of the head as she'd walked to the table. So, he must be working, but who, or what, was his interest?

She let her gaze slowly travel the room, smiling and nodding when she made eye contact with those she knew, and there were many, before her attention returned to Danvers.

"Are you here for anyone in particular?" he asked.

"Yes, you. It was your choice of restaurant, remember. I just wanted to see who was here."

"Lord save me from a nosy woman." He picked up his glass and stared at her over the rim. "You don't fool me for a minute, you know, but your presence will do my reputation no harm at all. A pity I can't say the same for yours."

Eleanor gulped her wine. "Let me solve this case first," she said. "Then I can worry about my reputation."

Chapter 19

The private club that Danvers took her to came as something of a surprise to Eleanor. She had expected something seedy, down at heel if not downright dirty, populated by gaunt-faced, hollow-eyed denizens risking everything on the roll of the dice or the turn of a card.

The Embassy, however, was no gambling den. Tucked away down a side street in Soho, the club was plush to the point of opulence.

The well-built seats were upholstered in velvet, the carpet deep-piled and the bar, made from highly polished walnut and brass, shone brightly under the glittering light of the chandeliers.

Eleanor saw many people she knew, peers of the realm and assorted aristocracy, members of Parliament from both sides of the house, and leaders of industry and commerce.

"Is it always this busy?"

"Always, my lady. Not that I come here that often, mind, and never in the company of such a beautiful woman."

"Less of the flattery, Danny boy. Do I have to buy chips or tokens?" Eleanor glanced around for a cash desk.

"Yes, you'll get them over here."

With Danny to squire her, Eleanor exchanged her money, then went to the bar and bought them both a drink. Despite her claim that morning, she asked for a cocktail.

"I could have got those," he protested, as she handed him a single malt whisky.

"Don't worry. You can get the next one."

He nodded and sipped at his drink. "You don't gamble then, my lady?"

"It isn't one of my vices, no. What about you?"

"On my salary? Fat chance."

"Yet, you know this place and have been here before," she pointed out.

"Ah, but on those occasions you might say that I was here on business. It's surprising where you get to when you're chasing a story. Besides, you don't have to gamble while you're here, though the owners would prefer that you did, naturally enough."

They wandered to the blackjack tables and watched the play for a while, but Eleanor's real interest lay in the players. So far, the person she had hoped to see was not in evidence.

"Is there another room?"

"More than one. What takes your fancy? Poker or roulette?"

Neither. As she had said, Eleanor was not a gambler. She was there on business, trying to prove an outrageous theory and bring a killer to justice. If it took a visit to a gambling club, then so be it. Her only concern was that she didn't lose too much money.

"My lady?" Danvers prompted.

Eleanor thought fast. Her quarry had neither the temperament, nor the face, for poker. "Oh, roulette I think."

"This way, then."

She followed him across the floor to a door in the wall. He tapped and it opened immediately. A broad shouldered doorman looked them up and down, then stepped back to let them in.

"That's odd, isn't it?" Eleanor whispered. "Why bother with a doorman? All they're after is your money, so why not let everybody just walk in?"

Danvers shrugged. "Ours not to reason why, fair lady, but I've seen some large sums staked in here. Maybe they want to be sure their clientele has the wherewithal before they're allowed to play."

Eleanor nodded as she quickly scanned the room, taking in the people around the two tables, shocked to see some famous faces, and quite a few acquaintances.

The noise levels were higher here than in the outer room as gamblers clacked their chips down, and the ivory ball rattled around the wheel and landed with a clunk that was greeted by cheers or groans.

The aroma of cigar smoke, the smell of perfume, the underlying sense of fear mingled with elation, and the buzz of excitement all left Eleanor feeling overwhelmed and longing to be home, in her quiet little flat, with only Tilly and a roaring fire for company.

At least her journey had not been in vain.

With a hawk-like gaze fastened on the wheel of the table closest to the door, Barbara Lancashire chewed at her lower lip. Beads of perspiration marked her forehead, her hands clenched and unclenched themselves in a ceaseless rhythm. Oblivious to anything other than that small white ball, she was unaware of Eleanor's presence or her scrutiny.

"Found what you were after?"

Danny Danvers rested his chin on Eleanor's shoulder. She inclined her head in response to his whisper, then turned away and stood watching the play on the second table.

Shortly after the war, Eleanor had lived in Paris, and still maintained an apartment there which she visited from time to time. On one occasion she had visited a casino and was instructed in the intricacies of betting in roulette, winning and losing in equal amounts. It had been a fun evening, but not one she had been at pains to repeat, though she was surprised at how much of the actual betting, and the odds, she remembered.

"Damn it all to hell! I need a drink."

A man opposite pushed himself away from the table and strode towards the door. His place was quickly filled by someone else.

"More money than sense, as my mother would say," Danvers muttered.

Eleanor smiled. "My maid says the same thing. She'd be horrified if she knew I was here."

"So, are you going to play or aren't you?"

"Perhaps. In a moment."

She walked to the other table. Barbara Lancashire still had a small amount of chips in front of her, though she appeared undecided where to place them. Eleanor wondered how many she had started with.

"Place your bets, ladies and gentlemen. Place your bets."

At the croupier's call arms stretched across the table, chips were placed hither and yon along the board, and the tension began to mount.

Barbara had placed two chips: one on All Red, the other on Black 17. If 17 came up, then she would win a tidy sum, but she wouldn't get so much from a red number. Hedging her bets, but too bitten by the gambling bug to cash in her chips and go home.

Eleanor chose a number and put her chips on the table.

"No more bets, ladies and gentlemen."

The croupier spun the wheel and the air around Eleanor seemed to electrify. Then he dropped the ball and the excitement grew as it clattered around past the spinning numbers. Time slowed. It seemed to take an age for the wheel to come to a halt and a mass exhalation greeted the arrival of the ball as it settled into slot number 10. Black 10.

Eleanor caught Barbara's muttered expletive and watched as the losing chips were skilfully raked away. Then the croupier counted out a stack of chips and pushed them to Eleanor.

"Place your bets, ladies and gentlemen. Place your bets."

As Eleanor picked up her winnings, she glanced across the table. Barbara Lancashire's eyes were like chips of ice. She almost snarled.

"Well done, your ladyship. I haven't seen you in here before."

"Yes." Eleanor gave a gay laugh. "Entirely beginner's luck. Now I'm away to my bed before I give it all back to them. Goodnight!"

With Danvers at her elbow, she re-entered the main room and headed for the cash desk.

"How much did you bet?"

"Oh, all of it." Eleanor threw him a teasing smile.

"And that was?"

There was no earthly reason why she should tell him, but he'd had enough decency to stand back when she had bought her chips and thus had no idea how much she'd paid out for them. If her memory of odds and payouts from that one occasion in Paris was not at fault, then the evening had proved worthwhile in more ways than one. She could, at least, let him share in the excitement of the moment.

"A hundred."

His eyebrows rose and he gave a low whistle. "Have you any idea how much you won?"

"Yes." By Eleanor's reckoning she was the richer by three thousand and six hundred pounds, and she had her original stake back, too.

"With your luck, I'd love to take you to Monte Carlo."

"But not tonight, though you can take me home."

Their taxi pulled up on the opposite side of the road to Bellevue Mansions. Telling the driver to wait, Danvers got out with her.

"Thank you for an enjoyable evening, Danny."

"Ach, you're welcome, though going out with you could make a man turn to drink — and thanks for the excellent claret, then whisky — though it would be a shame if he did." He touched her blonde hair, stroking the back of her head. "He'd miss so much that was fascinating, intriguing, and beautiful."

He pulled her to him and kissed her.

Eleanor neither struggled nor resisted, but kissed him just as firmly back, her arms going around his waist, holding the embrace.

She was breathless when they broke apart, but pushed him gently away. Always leave them wanting more was her maxim.

Besides, she had every intention of seeing him again, and the night had served its purpose.

With a light heart she crossed the road and climbed the steps. It was only by the merest chance, as she turned to call good night, that she caught sight of the lurker in the shadows. She shivered and hurried inside.

Chapter 20

The following morning brought a note from Ariadne Beresford with a list of her mother's guests on the night her emerald necklace had disappeared.

As expected, there were a number of guests who had also attended Barbara Lancashire's soirée. In the normal run of things, Eleanor would have put this down to coincidence, but one name attracted her particular attention.

She tapped the paper against her lips and shook her head. "I'm making mountains out of molehills and bricks without straw. Besides, jewel robberies can't have anything to do with Sir David's murder. Can they?"

It was strange how so little information regarding the robberies had leaked into the public domain. If Tommy and Sophie's guests were to be believed, then London was currently undergoing a spate of such thefts, yet Eleanor could not recall seeing anything of them in either the Times or the Daily Banner. Perhaps the unlucky owners had not reported their loss to the police, or the latter were keeping it quiet, for reasons best known to themselves.

Eleanor heaved a sigh. The answer would not be found sitting at Bellevue Mansions. It was time to do a disappearing act.

And obtain reinforcements.

In order not to be seen by the watcher out the front, she told Tilly she was going out and left the building by the rear door. Collecting the Lagonda, she drove first to see Ann.

"Where are we going?" Lady Ann drained her coffee cup and stared bleary-eyed at her friend. "You know I'm not a morning person."

"I thought we'd take a trip to the theatre."

"At this time in the morning? Don't be ridiculous."

"We are going to the Viceroy, but not to see a performance. The booking office will be open, so we can get in. Then, we are going to sit and think and wander around the circle."

"Wandering around in circles is about all my brain is good for." Ann poured more coffee. "Whatever do we need to go to the theatre for?" She gave Eleanor a keen look. "Are we sleuthing?"

"Yes."

"Well, why didn't you say so? If there's any sleuthing to be done, then I'm your girl." The coffee cup rattled onto the saucer. "Give me five minutes and I'll be with you."

It was nearer to half an hour before the Lagonda pulled away from outside Ann's front door, and Eleanor drove them to the West End.

Ann prattled for most of the way, wanting to know whether they were likely to see Deanna Dacre and what progress Eleanor was making in solving Sir David Bristol's murder.

"Oh, I doubt we'll see Miss Dacre. She won't be at the theatre this early. It's not as if they are rehearsing or anything. As to Bristol...well, I have a few ideas, most of them outlandish, and I'll admit that I'm baffled. It's been nearly a week and I don't even have a motive." Eleanor stamped a gloved fist on the steering wheel.

"Buck up, old chum. You're doing no worse than the police, by the looks of things. I keep reading the paper, expecting to see news of an arrest, and that our old friend Blount of Scotland Yard has been busy and laid the culprit by the heels. There's been nothing. Bristol's murder hasn't even been mentioned for a day or two."

Eleanor shrugged, concentrating on her driving. "Yes, a three-day wonder, but then, these jewel robberies haven't been mentioned at all. Have you heard of any more?"

"Well, only hearsay, but apparently even Mrs Henderson has reported stolen jewels."

"Mrs Henderson?"

"Yes, wife of Arthur Henderson, the Home Secretary. Whoa!" Ann hung onto her seat as the car swerved violently, then flung an arm wide to grab hold of Eleanor. "Steady on. Are you all right?"

"Sorry, yes. I didn't see that coming."

Ann twisted in her seat and looked back the way they had come. "What coming? I didn't see anything?"

The car's pace slackened as a grin spread across Eleanor's features. "Is Ariadne Beresford's father in the government or the Civil Service?"

"Hmm? Yes, yes I believe he is, now that you come to mention it. So what?"

"So, that's my link. Ooh, Ann, I could kiss you."

Panic rushed into Ann's eyes and she leaned against the door. "I'd really rather you didn't, darling, and certainly not at the moment. Just keep your mind on driving, all right?"

Eleanor laughed. "All right. It isn't far now, anyway. The Viceroy is just around the corner."

Inside the theatre's lobby, an elderly couple stood at the window of the booking office, enquiring after tickets for that evening's performance. Eleanor walked past them and tapped on the manager's door. It opened almost immediately and a dark head looked out.

"Yes?"

It took a moment for him to recognise Eleanor and his reaction was one of worry not welcome. She held out her card.

"I see that you remember me. I have been retained by Miss Deanna Dacre to investigate the tragic events of last week. With your permission" — she dipped her head — "I would like to have a look at the boxes that both Sir David, and my friend and I occupied at that time."

"But why?" he objected. "There is nothing to see. Besides, once the police had finished with it, Sir David's box has been sold every night to other theatregoers."

"Oh, I'm sure it has, but there is something I need to check on. We won't be long."

"Oh, very well, though I think you are wasting your time. I'll put the house lights on. Let me know when you have finished, please. I don't want them burning all day. We pay enough for electricity as it is."

He closed the door and Ann, much as she had done the previous week, slipped her arm through her friends as they headed for the stairs.

"Bit of a surly character, isn't he?" she remarked.

"Perhaps. I wonder what Bristol's murder has done for ticket sales."

"Normally, I would have said that they'd have gone through the roof —"

"Cynic!"

"— but I think they were doing that anyway. People have flocked to see Deanna Dacre acting her socks off. She's all the rage, and anyone who's anyone wants to see her."

Eleanor pushed open the doors at the top of the stairs and led the way into the lower circle.

"So, what do we do now we're here?" asked Ann.

Reaching into her bag, Eleanor took out a notebook, a pen, and a small stopwatch. "I want to time how long it would take someone to reach Sir David's box."

Ann looked appalled. "From where? If you intend tramping all over this place, then you needn't include me. I shall go for a snooze in the box that we had."

"Don't worry, lazybones." Eleanor smiled. "We are only going to walk half of the circle. It helps that Bristol was in the centre box, so the time would be the same from either end."

"You go. I'll stay here and wait for you."

Eleanor shook her head. "Honestly. All these parties have made you soft. All right, go into our box and I'll join you as soon as I can."

She turned her back on her friend, who was soon lost to view by the curve of the circle, and strode off to the left.

Ann was sitting in the front row of the box looking out over the empty auditorium and the curtained stage when Eleanor returned.

"Did that tell you anything?"

"I don't know. I walked it in both directions, just to be sure there were no impediments, but the time itself doesn't tell me very much."

"Yeah, the killer could have run. Or dawdled. Or come down from the upper circle. So, what was the point?"

Eleanor took the seat beside her friend and pulled at lower lip with thumb and forefinger.

"I'm just trying to cover all the angles. We know that Bristol died only a few minutes before the end of the second act, when everyone, save for the killer, was in their seats."

"Not necessarily." Ann wagged a finger. "People might have been heading for the restrooms or the bar, to get their drinks in early for the interval. There might have been any number of people around at that time."

"Well, that's possible, of course, but don't forget that Deanna was giving it her all on the stage at the time. We were all spellbound by her performance. It would have had to be a real emergency to have dragged anyone away before the curtain fell."

Ann remained unconvinced. "You were dragged away."

"Yes, but that's exactly my point. I thought there was an emergency in the next box."

"And you were right, as it turned out." Ann's tone was acerbic.

"Are you sitting in the same seat that you were in that night?"

Ann glanced about. "No, I think I was two seats to my left."

Eleanor asked her to move and then took her own seat against the wall.

"Now what?" Ann asked.

"Ignoring the stage, who did you notice in the other boxes?"

"Oh, Lor'!"

While Ann reeled off a list of names, Eleanor jotted them down in her notebook, then sat back and closed her eyes.

"What are you doing?"

"Shh! I'm trying to remember who I could see. Aah!" Eleanor's eyes snapped open. "You mentioned Robert and Barbara Lancashire. Are you sure you saw them both?"

Eleanor had a sudden vivid picture of Barbara — alone — sitting in the box closest to the left hand side of the stage, with one hand rubbing her right shoulder.

"Yes, I think so."

"Did you see Barbara rubbing her shoulder?"

"Lumme, what questions you ask."

"Yes, but did you? I wouldn't ask if it wasn't important."

"All right, darling, keep your hair on. Don't forget that I've been to sleep since then, and had a few cocktails, too."

Eleanor laughed. "Only a few?"

"Yeah, well, you know." Ann turned in her seat. "You know, you might be right. I'm not sure that Barbara was rubbing her shoulder, but she had her hand on it."

"Left hand on right shoulder, yes?" Eleanor struck up the same pose.

"Yes, exactly."

Was it all beginning to make sense?

Eleanor got to her feet. "Would you do me a favour and move into the box next door while I go and sit where I think Barbara was that night?"

"Uh uh." Much to Eleanor's surprise, her friend shuddered violently. "No, I know what you're up to, and I'll be Barbara if you don't mind. I just hope that the manager doesn't turn the lights out while I'm en-route."

The experiment proved worthwhile and Eleanor confessed herself well pleased as the two friends left the theatre and climbed back into the Lagonda.

"Well, I'm glad you think so." Ann settled back against the car's leather seat. "What does it all mean, though?"

"I'll tell you in a day or so, when I've worked it out myself."

"What? You mean you still don't know who killed Bristol?"

"Oh, I didn't say that." Eleanor glanced behind her, then pulled away into the London traffic. "But it's very complicated, and these jewel thefts everyone's been talking about have something to do with it."

"Then you'd better solve it quickly, and would you drop me in Bond Street, please? I must do some clothes shopping. I don't have a thing to wear."

"Ha! Darling, you tell fibs. Honestly, Ann Carstairs, you've enough clothes to dress a small army."

"Ah, but only if they wore tatters."

Eleanor let Ann out at the top of Bond Street and drove back along Piccadilly with only half a mind on her driving. The other half was busy elsewhere.

She went back to the beginning of the whole affair. It had started when Barbara Lancashire had engaged her to find a necklace. Only a matter of days later, in which time Eleanor had learned a lot about both Barbara and her stolen property, the commission had been cancelled, yet she continued to hear of other thefts.

Now, it seemed, all the jewellery had been taken from the homes of Government Ministers and Civil Servants. Oh, except for Scarletti the opera singer's tiara. So, perhaps that was unconnected.

The significance of this, taken in conjunction with the case that currently engaged the Major, did not escape her. How, though, were the two things related?

And what of Danny Danvers? Was he involved in any way?

Eleanor hoped not. With that easy going charm he'd spoken of, he made an agreeable companion, though his flattery could prove tiresome. Besides, said a niggling voice inside her, he wasn't the man she really wanted to spend time with, or kiss with the passion she'd expended on the reporter.

And the man in the shadows? Time to return to Bellevue Mansions, and hope there had been a message from her young scout.

Chapter 21

No one had seen or heard from Joe when Eleanor returned home. The doorman was adamant that the young newsboy hadn't been around, not even to sell his papers.

"These urchins are all the same, if you ask me, my lady. They come and they go. Doubt you'll see him again."

Tilly said much the same thing.

"You can't expect young Joe to be outside at all hours, my lady, and you were late home last night. You might have imagined that someone was outside, or he could have had a reason for being there."

"Don't cluck over me, Tilly. If I wanted to live with my mother I'd go home to Rowsley Park. And I did not imagine it."

Tilly shrugged, used to this recurring difference of opinion between them. "Besides," she said, "Joe has probably just taken your money and scarpered."

That thought had occurred to Eleanor, and it was not one she cared to dwell on. No man made a fool of Eleanor Bakewell, especially when he was only eleven years old, and grimy to boot. She wasn't prepared to give up on the boy so easily, though.

"He may have done, but I'm still worried."

She ate a small piece of smoked salmon for lunch, then left the apartment block to collect the Lagonda again.

The previous evening's lurker was not in evidence, but the street was busy with folk going about their daily business, anyone of whom might have replaced him. Whoever had her under surveillance might have a day and a night shift, with several men at their disposal to have her, and the building, permanently watched.

She shuddered at the thought and stamped on the car's accelerator, sending it speeding down Piccadilly, heading east towards Fleet Street.

Her intention of asking the Daily Banner's receptionist for information regarding their distribution depot was thwarted by her running into Danny Danvers on the pavement outside the building.

"Good morning, my lady. A pleasure to see you again." His eyes twinkled. "Can I hope that, swayed by my company and my easy-going charm yesterday evening, you were coming to see me? Perhaps you'd like me to kiss you again."

Eleanor smiled in return. "Sadly not, and not in broad daylight in the middle of Fleet Street. I came looking for information about your paperboys."

He raised an eyebrow. "Not had your paper delivered this morning? That's subscriptions. You'll find them on the second floor, though a simple phone call would have done the job."

"No, it's not that. I would like to know where the delivery boys get their copies from before they go hawking them on the streets."

Danny gazed at her sternly. "May I ask why? It's seems an odd thing to concern a lady like yourself." He took a step towards her. "Is everything all right?"

She shook her head and debated how much to take him into her confidence. "I don't know."

"Has this anything to do with your investigation into Bristol's murder? Though what paperboys have to do with that I can't imagine. Still, you know your own business. It's a bit of a comedown, though, from high-rollers in posh gaming clubs to urchins delivering the Daily Banner. What's your interest?"

The worry gnawing away inside Eleanor got the better of her. "Danny, will you please just answer the question? I need to know where the papers are handed to the boys. Where do they collect them?"

He held up a placatory hand. "All right. I'm sorry, I didn't realise it was so serious. The delivery outlet is just around the corner here in Wilton Street." He pointed along the road. "Turn right, then second left. You'll see a building with a large open forecourt and a sign saying Daily Banner."

She held out her hand. "Thank you."

Danny caught hold of it and raised it to his lips. "You're welcome. Let me know if I can help, won't you? Murder's a foul business — and a dangerous one. I hate to think of someone as beautiful as yourself being involved and at risk."

"Thank you," she said again. "Your concern is duly noted, but I can take care of myself. However, I'll call you if there's anything you can do."

She turned on her heel and got back into the Lagonda, waving to him as she drew away from the kerb.

The place Danny had directed her to was easily found and she parked again and went inside.

A veritable hive of activity met her gaze as men bustled around carrying bundles of newspapers from somewhere in the rear to a fleet of waiting delivery vans all painted in the Daily Banner's livery.

She stopped the first person she saw.

"Excuse me, I'm trying to find Joe Minshull. Do you know him?"

The worker nodded. "Oh, aye, everyone knows Joe."

"Has he been in today?"

"I can't say, ma'am." He turned away and yelled at the rest of the workforce. "Anyone seen young Joe Minshull today?"

A chorus of negatives greeted the question and he turned back to Eleanor.

"Sorry, ma'am. You could try asking Bill Dean, the foreman. He's in that office over there."

She followed his pointing figure to a small poky room fashioned out of the greater space by the addition of three sections of lath and plasterboard and a single pane of glass. The occupant of the cabin would have the men outside under surveillance at all times.

Eleanor knocked and went in.

"Yes, madam? May I help you?" A squat, thickset man in a brown workcoat looked up as she pushed open the door.

"Mr Dean?"

He nodded.

"Good morning. I'm sorry to bother you." Eleanor handed over her business card. "I'm looking for one of your delivery boys, Joe Minshull. Do you know him, and have you seen him lately?"

The man glanced at the card, eyes widening, and handed it back. "Well now, Lady Bakewell, I've no idea what concern it is of yours, but it's funny you should say that. I haven't seen Joe for a day or two, and that's strange, 'cause he's usually very reliable."

"Would you also say that he was honest?"

He scratched his crooked nose with a blackened finger, leaving a streak of newsprint down one side. "As the day is long. His money always matches to the penny and I've never had cause to doubt him."

Eleanor frowned. "Then I wonder where he is."

A shrug. "He could be sick, I suppose. The boys work for themselves and don't have to clock in or anything. The union is trying to change that, get them some security like, but the management don't want to know."

"Oh? I thought your last owner, Sir David Bristol, was a socialist, on the side of the working man. Or boy. Was that not so?"

His mouth took on a sardonic twist. "Only if he's already earning a goodly sum, if your ladyship will forgive me saying so. Bristol and his cronies are only playing at being socialists and giving it lip service, in my opinion. They may have wanted the state to own everything, but if so it was only so they could strip it bare for their own benefit and to line their own pockets."

Having delivered himself of a viewpoint that Eleanor was coming to suspect was the truth, he sat back and crossed his hands behind his head, looking at her as though daring her to contradict him.

Eleanor did nothing of the sort. It was a conversation she would have loved to continue — she had, after all, been retained to solve the mystery of Bristol's death — but her main concern, at the moment, was to find Joe.

"Do you happen to know where Joe lives? If so, I would be grateful for his address, please."

Dean looked down again at Eleanor's card. "Joe's not in any trouble, is he? He's always seemed a good lad. One who kept his nose clean, as it were."

Except when it was blackened by newsprint, Eleanor thought, looking at Dean's own nose.

"I sincerely hope not, Mr Dean, and not in the way you mean, but I am concerned about his welfare. If he is that sick that he cannot work, then..."

Let him draw his own conclusions from that unfinished sentence. She tapped her foot on the floor.

"Well, your ladyship, you'll understand that it isn't usual to give out the addresses of our employees."

"But, Joe isn't one of the Banner's employees, is he? Not strictly speaking, and you've admitted as much yourself." She placed her hands on the paper strewn desk and leant towards him, eyes softening. "Please, Mr Dean. I only want to help Joe."

Whether it was the pleading look, or the soft voice that did it, Eleanor was never to know, but the foreman got up from his chair and went to a filing cabinet. He lifted out a folder and began to rifle through it.

"As I recall, the Minshulls have rooms in Cook Place. It's not far from here, on the opposite side of Fleet Street." He turned over a few more scraps of paper. "Ah, here we are. The Minshulls are at number 5."

"Thank you." Eleanor was out of the office before the filing drawer had closed.

Cook Place, when she eventually found it, turned out to be a ramshackle row of old cottages that even the Victorians, with their zeal for cleanliness and good sanitation, had failed to pull down, although someone ought to have done so, in Eleanor's estimation. Little more than hovels, their tiled roofs leaned together like a party of drunks on the way home from the pub.

Gripped by a strong temptation to turn and flee, Eleanor had to steel herself to rap on the door. It was opened by a child with a surprisingly clean face wearing ragged trousers held up by string. His too big shirt was frayed at cuff and collar.

"Hello." Eleanor smiled down at a younger version of her quarry. "Is Joe at home?"

"No."

He made to close the door, but Eleanor got her foot in the opening. "Do you know where he is?"

"No."

"When did you last see him?"

"Dunno. A day or so ago."

"Who is it, Georgie?" A quavering female voice called out from inside. "Who's there?"

The child addressed as Georgie turned his head and looked back into the room. "A lady."

Eleanor stepped inside, pushing the boy gently to one side. "Mrs Minshull? Forgive the intrusion, but may I come in and speak to you for a moment, please?"

Propped up on one elbow, a middle-aged woman lay on a mattress next to a small fireplace. A threadbare blanket covered her and she plucked at it fitfully as she stared up at the visitor.

The grate was largely bare of coal and the fire gave off smoke but little warmth into the cold, damp room. Black mould spread its disgusting fingers along the top of one wall, and Eleanor shuddered despite herself.

"It looks like you already have done." Mrs Minshull coughed and clutched a scrap of fabric to her mouth. She took a sip from a glass of water on the floor beside the mattress. "Blimey! I thought our Joe were tellin' porkies when he said he'd met a lady. Were it you he were talking about?"

"Your son told you the truth, Mrs Minshull. I'm Lady Eleanor Bakewell."

"Yeah, that was the name. Wotcha want?"

"I'm looking for Joe."

"Ha! You and me both!" A fit of coughing racked her frame and she collapsed back exhausted onto the bed. "I haven't seen him in three days. Don't know where he is or what's happened to him and I got the 'flu so bad I can't go looking for him neither." She raised a pair of piteous, red rimmed eyes to Eleanor. "Gawd help us all."

"Does Joe always come home?"

"Yes, always. He's a good lad is our Joe. I lost his dad in the war when Georgie was only a baby. Joe considers himself the man of the family, now, an' does his best to look after us all."

Mrs Minshull coughed and lay back, the effort of speech clearly tiring her.

Eleanor looked around her in despair, unable to shift the feeling that Joe's disappearance was somehow her fault and that she had to make amends.

"I'm going to fetch a doctor," she announced, and all hell broke loose, as the woman on the mattress screamed and the youngster started to cry.

Chapter 22

Eleanor calmed Mrs Minshull's cries that she could not afford a doctor or a hospital, by the simple expedient of paying for the former herself.

Dr Laverick was a kindly, elderly man, who examined Joe's mother thoroughly, divested himself of the opinion that a change of living accommodation and diet would do wonders for the health of most of the capital's poor, and finally diagnosed a mild bout of influenza.

"I know that." Mrs Minshull wheezed. "I just can't afford no medicine."

"I can," said Eleanor, and handed over the doctor's fee in return for a prescription.

"Should I take her to a hospital?"

The doctor shook his head. "I doubt it's that severe, but she really needs to to be in the warm and dry."

Eleanor fetched the medicine, bought a bag of groceries, arranged for a delivery of coal and returned to the sick woman.

"Do you have a job, Mrs Minshull?"

She took a sticky bun out of the grocery bag and offered it to Georgie. The child's eyes widened, but it looked to its mother first, and only with her nod of approval did he take the treat from Eleanor's hand.

"Fank you."

"I did have, but I lost my job when I fell sick. Look, I'm grateful, an' all, but why are you doin' all this? What's in it for you?"

"I need you to get well." Eleanor pulled her coat closer and hugged the collar to her neck. "Then I'll have a proposition to put to you. I would move you and your child from here right now, but that won't help Joe if he comes back and you're not here."

"An' what if he don't come back?"

Eleanor's stomach churned and she clenched her jaw. "He will. I'll find him." She took a ten-shilling note from her bag and pushed it into the woman's hand. "I'll be back in a day or two. Take care of yourself."

She drove home with her mind in turmoil and with a hot flush of anger burning deep inside her. All well and good to tell his mother that she would find Joe, but how was she to do that when she had no idea where he might be?

Resisting the temptation to accost the lurker outside her building and ask him what had happened to the paperboy, she entered Bellevue Mansions as she had left it — by the rear door.

"How can we call ourselves a civilised country, Tilly, when people are living in such dire conditions? Going into Cook Place was like stepping back into the Middle Ages."

"I don't know, my lady, and you can't right every wrong. You did what you could for her. Most people wouldn't have bothered."

Eleanor shook her head. "Surely, I only did what any caring person would do for a fellow human being?"

Tilly sniffed. "Well, if it's Christian charity you're after giving, then you should join the Church."

"Do you think I did wrong?" Eleanor reached for a cigarette. "I'm worried about Joe."

"It's not my place to say, but if you want my opinion, then you did do the right thing. And you've no call to blame yourself over that young man."

Tilly's attempt to console her mistress left Eleanor in deeper gloom. She sat with her thoughts for over an hour, wondering what to do for the best, and was none too pleased at the arrival of a visitor.

"Major Armitage is here to see you, my lady. Shall I tell him you're out?"

Eleanor groaned. "No, you'd better show him in, please, Tilly, and perhaps you'd better make us a pot of coffee."

Armitage looked tired when he entered, the fine lines at eye and mouth more deeply etched. Eleanor was in no mood to offer him tender care, however.

"There's a man out there watching the front of this building. Is he one of yours?"

The major, blinking at her abruptness, shook his head and crossed to the window. "No. Despite what you may think of me, my lady, I'm not having you watched." He stood behind the curtain, staring at the stretch of pavement opposite, then craning his neck to see below. "How long has he been there?"

"I don't know. I noticed him for the first time last night."

"After your evening out with Danny Danvers, you mean?"

Eleanor's eyes narrowed. "Yes, though I hardly think that has anything to do with it, nor are my escorts any concern of yours." She waved him to a seat. "Do you know that man?"

"I can't say that I do. Perhaps he's one of your many admirers."

He smiled and the tiredness dropped from his face. If her mood had been brighter she might have encouraged the teasing and the banter. As it was she ignored it.

"So, what can I do for you, Major?"

"I was wondering if you had made any progress with Bristol's murder?"

"Ha! Chance would be a fine thing."

"Is it as bad as all that?" He spoke softly, and a gentle smile curved his lips.

Eleanor felt her own lips begin to tremble and was saved from bursting into tears by the arrival of her maid with the coffee tray.

"It feels like it, especially today." She turned to Tilly. "Will you pour, please."

She stood and reached down the cigarette box from the mantelpiece and offered it to her visitor. He took one, and lit hers before his own.

Eleanor resumed her seat with a brief word of thanks. "Everything is so jumbled up that if you're expecting coherent thinking, then you've come to the wrong place and the wrong person."

He smiled. "Why don't you let me be the judge of that? Tell me what you suspect. Perhaps if we put our heads together we can make sense of it."

She wrinkled her nose, loath to commit herself whilst still unsure. Would he think her a fool? At least he wouldn't laugh at her if he did.

"All right. Barbara Lancashire retained my services to retrieve a stolen pearl necklace with a distinctive clasp. There have been a spate of jewel robberies in London recently. She is also an inveterate gambler and I suspect that heavy losses on the gaming table have left her in debt."

"Hmm. Not what you want in the wife of a man with as much responsibility as Sir Robert. Go on."

Eleanor picked up her coffee cup and took a sip. "Well, it is my belief that Bristol was blackmailing her over these debts, possibly threatening to make them public, though I don't know if that was the reason for his death. Nor do I think he was blackmailing her for money."

"Ah." Armitage finished his cigarette, threw the butt in the fire, and leaned towards her, hands clasped between his knees.

"The day after Bristol's death," Eleanor went on, "Barbara asked me to call on her and told me she no longer required my services. She gave me some cock-and-bull story about having forgotten that she'd sent the necklace to be cleaned."

"And you think that he wanted the necklace?"

Eleanor shook her head. "No, I think he wanted information, and the way she passed that information to him was by wearing the necklace."

There! She'd said it. Now let him think her a fool.

Armitage scratched at his furrowed brow. "I'm sorry, Eleanor, I don't quite see..."

"Look, a string of pearls is usually long enough to go over the head, or it has a clasp that fastens on the back of the neck. Barbara's however were unique in having a clasp that was designed to be worn on either shoulder. If you are right about Bristol being the leader of a spy ring, and needing to know which of two days Monsieur Doumergue would be at Chequers, then this was a way to tell him."

"I see. So, right shoulder Wednesday, left shoulder Thursday, that sort of thing?"

"Yes, exactly that. So, with the theft of her pearls, Barbara sat in her box at the Viceroy with her left hand on her right shoulder."

"This was the night that Bristol was murdered?"

"Yes, I spotted her and thought at first that she was rubbing her shoulder, as if it were sore. Lady Ann Carstairs noticed it, too. We went back to the Viceroy yesterday, and...er...compared notes."

The major's lips twitched into the familiar quirky smile. "Glad to see you're as thorough as always."

Eleanor shrank back. "I'm not playing at this. Don't forget that Deanna Dacre is employing me to solve Bristol's murder. I intend to do just that."

"Don't be so jumpy, my lady. I meant it as a compliment."

She shrugged and drank more coffee before replacing cup and saucer on the table at her side. "I take it *you* know when Mr Doumergue will meet with Mr MacDonald? Because, you see, we still don't know which day Barbara was indicating."

"Oh, quite, quite. Nor do we know who else is in this group of spies, though we are keeping a close eye on the two names you gave me earlier. Have you heard anything else? I don't have to remind you that time is ticking away."

"No, Major, you don't." She helped herself to another cigarette and debated whether to tell him about Joe. The boy's disappearance bothered her. It had to have something to do with this spy business. If he'd simply taken her money and run, then he would not have been missing from work or from home — and he would not have got far on a single shilling.

She smiled to herself at the memory of his face as he looked at the shiny coin, and of how he'd refused it in favour of one of Tilly's breakfasts. Tears welled in her eyes and she brushed them away with an angry hand. If any harm had come to that boy, she might commit murder herself.

"My lady? Eleanor?"

Armitage's quiet voice broke into her thoughts. Clamping down on emotions that threatened to overwhelm her, she cursed her weakness, and drew on her cigarette. "Well, going back to what I said earlier, I wonder if it is possible that the jewel thefts are the work of your spies, and the money raised is being used to fund their activities."

He seemed surprised by the suggestion, but gave it due consideration.

"Perhaps, but the likes of Bristol had deep pockets, anyway. Why go to the trouble of stealing jewellery?"

"Because, Major, one gets deep pockets by spending other people's money and not one's own. Of course, the thief could be one of the gang and still be lining his own pockets, the thefts having nothing to do with his espionage activity. Do you suppose spy rings have accountants?"

He laughed. "Doubt it. How they get their money is a minor issue, however. We still don't know when they plan to assassinate Monsieur Doumergue, or where their hideout is?"

"David Bristol's office in Bromwich Street would be a good place to start, wouldn't it?"

Eleanor gave her visitor a long hard stare. How much more did he expect her to do? She had passed on all her suspicions, all the information that might be relevant, everything she had gleaned about Bristol's death, and the antics of the wife of a government minister.

In the process she had found herself watched and possibly put the life of a small boy at risk. Enough was enough.

She was about to say so when he forestalled her.

"We've had someone in Bromwich Street for a while. It's the main reason that we knew what Bristol was up to. I know I said before that his death had done us a favour, but on reflection, it hasn't. We're now in the dark. We don't know who has taken his place as the leader of the group or what their plans are."

"But you do," Eleanor protested. "Barbara Lancashire knows which day the Frenchman will be at Chequers, as does her husband. Go and speak to her, interrogate her, or whatever it is you do, and get her to tell you what information she — oh!"

Only now did it sink in that whatever Barbara had attempted to pass on to Bristol had never reached the spy ring. His murder had broken the chain.

And now she knew who had killed him.

Chapter 23

Major Armitage eventually took his leave and Tilly served a late lunch. Eleanor insisted her maid stayed with her, and while she ate, outlined her plans for the Minshull family. Tilly clucked and sniffed, but agreed that the plan was a good one.

She made a note of the Minshulls' address and agreed to go and see them.

"When do you want me to go to Bakewell House, my lady? I could do that after I've been to Cook Place."

"No, that's all right. We'll go together and do it tomorrow. I'm off to the Houses of Parliament this afternoon, I'm inviting myself to a party this evening and I'm going to impose myself on Penelope Studley-Gore. I'll wear the black dress, I think, and the diamond and feather headdress."

With these details sorted, she drove to the seat of British government in Westminster and wandered into the magnificent St Stephen's Hall, the main entrance to the Houses of Parliament.

Her father was a member here, with a seat in the House of Lords, though he preferred to stay on his estate and only turned up at the House on rare occasions. The duke maintained that his attendance was largely a waste of time. He always said that he got more sense out of his Russian wife and his sheep than out of any politician.

Eleanor smiled at the thought and was looking up at the hall's stupendous wooden roof, admiring the curve of its great oaken beams, when she heard her name being called.

"Lady Eleanor! Hello!"

"Oh, hello Mr Danvers."

"Fancy meeting you here, and twice in one day, not that it isn't always a pleasure to see you, my lady." He winked at her, his eyes alive with mischief. "Have you come for the speech?"

"Speech? What speech?"

"Didn't you know? Gerald Hope-Weedon is supposed to be making a speech this afternoon. The gossip is, he's supposed to be attacking his own leader over his refusal to appoint a Foreign Secretary. Some say he's after the job for himself."

Eleanor took a step back and gazed up at him. He seemed like a child, buzzing with excitement.

"But what does that have to do with you?" she asked. "I thought you were a crime reporter."

"Ha! According to my editor, if there is crime in London it's to be found right here, so I might as well be put to dashed use by covering this speech and killing two birds with one stone. Frankly, I think it's a crime that I've not made Chief Reporter yet, but my brilliance obviously escapes them."

"Poor you," she sympathised, and laughed.

"Ah, but I wouldn't be so poor if you'd accompany me to the press gallery, my lady." He doffed an imaginary hat and bowed low.

Eleanor was still laughing. "You do know how to show a girl a good time, Mr Danvers. Yes, all right, why not?"

He offered her his arm and she crooked a hand around his elbow as they walked through the long hall and up the stairs at the end. There were several more flights before they reached the press gallery and took their seats overlooking the chamber of the House of Commons.

A member was already on his feet and addressing the House, though Eleanor paid him little attention as she scanned the faces below and noted Mr MacDonald, and Gerald Hope-Weedon on the government side and Stanley Baldwin on the other.

Danvers took out his reporter's notebook and a pencil and began scribbling while Eleanor looked about her. News of Hope-Weedon's supposed speech had clearly spread, for both the press gallery, and the public gallery behind it, were full.

The proceedings soon bored Eleanor who had little time for politics and still less for politicians. The constant drawl of, "hear, hear, hear", was like the bleating of her father's sheep and grated on her nerves. She rubbed at her temples, feeling a headache starting to build behind her eyes.

When Hope-Weedon stood up to speak, he made no reference to foreign affairs, but instead made much of the plight of the poor. His cogent arguments and impassioned rhetoric made him a good speaker and despite her dislike of the man, Eleanor owned to being impressed.

"Was this what you were expecting?" she whispered to her companion.

He leaned his shoulder against hers, his mouth close to her ear. "Hardly. This isn't what brought the news hounds here. They were expecting something very different."

"Then I wonder why he changed his mind?"

Danvers continued to lean against her, his hot breath tickling her neck. "Who knows? There may be fireworks yet."

Unfortunately, there weren't, and after fifteen minutes Hope-Weedon sat down again.

Eleanor mulled over what he had said, her mind still full of Joe and his whereabouts.

All well and good for the high-and-mighty to pontificate about poverty as Hope-Weedon had just done, but what was he, or any member of parliament, doing about the likes of Cook Place? The whole street ought to be levelled and better houses built to replace them, with indoor sanitation, and electric lighting. No doubt some grasping landlord was still charging Mrs Minshull an exorbitant rent.

"Well, that was a surprise." Danvers flipped his notebook shut and got to his feet. "Care to join me for a spot of tea? There's a nice little tea house the other side of Parliament Street."

"Is there any chance of getting to speak to Mr Hope-Weedon, do you think?"

He shook his head. "Shouldn't think so. He'll be in the Chamber for a while longer, yet."

"In that case, yes I would like some tea."

With the absence of the expected sensation, the press gallery was thinning out, leaving only the true political correspondents behind. Eleanor and Danvers threaded their way between the seats and back down the stairs.

"Sorry that Weedon's speech turned into a disappointment," said Danvers, when they reached the outside. "Still, it means I get to treat you to tea, so it's not all bad news. By the way, did you find what you were looking for this morning? A missing youngster, wasn't it?"

"No, I didn't. I found the hovel where he lives, and I found his sick mother, but no sign of Joe. I have to admit to feeling worried for him."

"Oh, he'll turn up. Kids always do."

Eleanor was not so sanguine. She could not dismiss the subject as easily as the reporter, but she said nothing as he ushered her inside the Albemarle Tea Room. Warm, snug, and gaily decorated, it had several free tables and a smiling waitress bustled up as soon as they had taken their seats.

"So, how is your investigation into Bristol's death going?" Danvers asked when they were alone. "You haven't forgotten that you've promised me the story, have you?"

"Not at all. I'm pretty certain that I know the culprit."

"You do?" He leaned across the table, at the same time struggling with his notebook which he was attempting to withdraw from an inside pocket of his coat.

Eleanor held up a hand. "Not so fast. I said before that the police will be the first to know, not you. You'll have to wait your turn. Besides, I don't quite have all the facts, yet." She took a cigarette case and lighter from her bag and, in an apparent change of subject, said, "So, what did you make of Hope-Weedon? Do you know much about him?"

A quick shake of his dark head. "Can't say that I do. To be honest, politicians bring me out in hives and I usually avoid them like the plague. If it wasn't for my editor insisting I go along, you wouldn't get me within a mile of that place."

She laughed. "You'd have to do some interesting detours then, given where you work. You're within a mile of it nearly all day, every day."

Danvers gave a lop-sided grin. "Yeah, well. You get my gist."

The waitress arrived with a tray of tea and buttered crumpets which she placed in front of Eleanor.

"Ha!" said Danvers. "You're obviously expected to be mother."

"Heaven forfend."

"You don't want children?"

"Not for the foreseeable future, no."

His determination to put their relationship on a more personal footing was beginning to irk her. While his good looks and obvious charm were appealing, and she would normally have enjoyed the banter, she did not have the luxury of time for fooling around. Maybe Peter Armitage's sense of urgency had rubbed off on her.

She poured the tea and offered him the plate of crumpets.

"Now, tell me what you know of these jewel robberies?" she demanded.

He blinked and nearly dropped the plate. "Bejabers, is it always about work with you? Can't you relax, even for a minute?"

She sat back and picked up her teacup, cradling it to her with both hands. Her mother would disapprove — the duchess believed that cups should only be held by the handle between thumb and forefinger — but Eleanor didn't care. Mother was two hundred miles away.

"I'm sorry, Danny, and no, I can't really be as carefree as you want me to be. I have a murderer and a missing boy to find. I told you before that I'm not playing at this."

"You can say that again."

"Look, if it makes you feel any better, once this case is finished and I've given you your scoop, then we'll go out together and paint the town red. What about it?"

He waved a finger at her. "Be careful. I shall hold you to that. Now let me eat this crumpet whilst it's still hot."

Only when he'd eaten and drunk his fill did he return to the question she'd posed him.

"I've been hearing about these robberies for a day or so. Not surprisingly, most people are reluctant to talk about it. By my reckoning there have been at least half a dozen in almost as many days, and they usually take place when there are guests in the house."

"Yes, that's my understanding, too."

"So it's unlikely to be the servants that are responsible."

"Do you know any fences, Danny?"

"No, but I've opened a fair few gates in my time." He grinned, and was instantly apologetic. "Sorry. Not playing, you said. Right?"

Eleanor nodded.

"Well, strictly speaking, as acting as a fence is a criminal activity, then if I knew any I should tell the police. However, there's a pawnbroker on the Edgeware Road, who isn't too fussy what he takes in, or where it came from. Name of Hobson, as I recall."

"Thank you. I may drop by there tomorrow and try and get him to talk."

"Uh huh? Would you like company? I'm prepared to be your back up?"

Eleanor was considering the offer and about to accept — at the very least it would do no harm to have a witness — until he added, "The lady sits on the fence. It would make for a great story, and an even better headline."

"Thanks for the offer. I'll think about it and let you know."

And if she went at all, she would take Tilly, not some story-hungry reporter.

Chapter 24

Eleanor went home with every intention of committing a breach of etiquette and turning up, uninvited, at a friend's party. Luckily, a phone call from Ann saved her from this solecism.

"Hello, darling. Did I tell you I've organised a last minute party for Penelope Studley-Gore?"

"Yes, you did."

"Oh, good, because I'm inviting you as my guest. Your man of interest is going to be there and it would give you a chance to work your wiles on him."

"Oh?" Eleanor frowned. "And who might that be?"

"Gerald Hope-Weedon."

About to refuse — two lots of Weedon in one day constituted a surfeit in her estimation — Eleanor changed her mind.

"Yes, all right, thanks. I'll meet you there though, Ann. I'm going to call in on Barbara Lancashire on the way."

"Rather you than me." Ann's tinkling laugh rang out. "I'll see you there, then."

To say that her erstwhile client was not pleased to see Eleanor was an understatement. She wasted no time in telling her so.

"Really, Lady Eleanor, this is most inconvenient. What on earth you want at this time of an evening I can't imagine. Sir Robert and I have barely finished dinner, and I do not take kindly to the interruption."

Her face had turned puce and the puckered mouth closed with a snap.

Eleanor, however had no time for her ladyship's tantrums.

"How long had Sir David Bristol been blackmailing you?"

Barbara let out a squawk and sank, deflated, into an armchair with a hand to her throat, as if it was searching for the pearls that weren't there.

"How...how did you know?"

"A simple matter of putting two and two together."

"Please," Barbara put out a hand. "You won't tell Robert, will you?"

Eleanor shook her head. "I see no reason to. I presume it was over your gambling debts. Did it start at Menton? Did you have losses at the casino in Monte Carlo?"

"Yes." Barbara wrung and twisted her hands, an abject figure. "Robert doesn't know, though. I managed to keep it from him."

"Bristol threatened to make your debts public?"

"Yes, in that rag of his, the Daily Banner."

"And he demanded the necklace in exchange for keeping you out of the papers?"

A subtle change came over Lady Lancashire as Eleanor spoke, and an odd smile played around her lips. A look that might have been relief flashed in her eyes and was gone in an instant.

Relief at what? That her secret was out and that she no longer had to suffer blackmail? Or was it that the idea Eleanor had discussed with Armitage was correct?

"You do realise though, don't you, that it gives you a motive for his murder."

"Me? I did nothing of the sort."

"No, but from where you sat in your box at the Viceroy you could see who did."

Barbara cast her eyes down again. "I'm afraid not. I was looking at the stage." She looked up. "I have explained that to a constable from Scotland Yard. He said he was asking everyone in a box at the Viceroy that night if they had seen anything. Ha! Ridiculous. No one could take their eyes off Deanna Dacre."

"You didn't hear the shot?"

"Certainly not."

Eleanor was still puzzling over things when she arrived at Penelope Studley-Gore's party, but put a bright smile on her face as she embraced her hostess.

"You've obviously fully recovered from the 'flu, I'm glad to see. I hope you don't mind me inviting myself to your guest list, although Ann Carstairs must take most of the blame."

"Not at all, darling, I'm delighted to see you. How's the sleuthing business? I've been reading a lot of the Sherlock Holmes stories lately, and started to think of you when I do."

"Good heavens, I hope not." Eleanor laughed. "I don't look good in a deer-stalker and as for smoking a pipe...ugh."

"Did you manage to speak to Marjorie Arbuthnot? Was she any use to you?"

"Yes to both of those, and thank you for pointing me in her direction."

"Oh, you're more than welcome. I'm glad I was able to help. Well, come in. I'm sure there are plenty of people here that you know. Make yourself at home. The drinks are in the dining room which is where I suspect you'll find Ann."

She drifted away to speak to other guests and Eleanor glanced around for her quarry, then having spotted him, wandered into the dining room for a drink.

As Penny had suggested, many of the faces of those clustered around the long table at the rear of the room were familiar to Eleanor. She chatted amiably for a while, nibbling on olives, drinking a cocktail, and listening to all the society gossip.

No one mentioned jewel thefts, and even the murder of so notable a character as Sir David Bristol was ignored. The talk was all of fashion, jazz musicians, cars, and forthcoming parties.

Feeling old, Eleanor left them to it and went back into the main room looking for Ann.

With the exception of a settee and a smattering of upright chairs, most of the furniture that had made the room feel so overstuffed on Eleanor's previous visit had been moved out.

Gerald Hope-Weedon leaned against the wall next to the fireplace smoking a cigarette and talking to a man in a dark suit.

"I fear that MacDonald is an idealist and doesn't have a clue. Mark my words, Baldwin will be back in power by the end of the year."

"Naturally, we shall do our best to prevent that." Hope-Weedon sounded his usual smug self.

Eleanor groaned inwardly. She hated politics, but that was what this case was all about. If she was to solve a murder for Deanna Dacre, and help Major

Armitage catch his spies, then she had to put up with political talk and politicians.

She stepped closer, deliberately putting herself in the eyeline of the man in the dark suit, Penelope's husband, Sir Peregrine Studley-Gore.

"Hello, Lady Eleanor. Has Penny sent you to tell me off?" He smiled at her before turning back to his companion. "Penny hates it when I talk politics, but what else is there to talk about to a politician, eh? Ha ha."

"Not at all, Perry." Eleanor returned his smile. "Your secret is safe with me."

"Good-oh, what? Do you know Mr Gerald Hope-Weedon, my lady?"

"Yes, we have met." She held out a hand to the politician, and suppressed a shiver as he raised to it his lips.

"Ah, yes, Lady Eleanor Bakewell. A pleasure to meet you again, Lady Eleanor."

"Thank you. That was quite a speech you gave in the House today, Mr Hope-Weedon."

"You were there? Oh, and please call me Gerald."

"Yes, I was. I thought, though, that you were attached to the Foreign and not the Home Office."

He raised an eyebrow. "Well, yes, but that doesn't stop me speaking out on matters of social inequality and injustice."

"And what do you propose to do about that?"

"Yes, Weedon," Sir Peregrine put in. "They say the poor will always be with us. What can your party do to change that?"

"Better and more affordable housing, perhaps?" asked Eleanor, remembering Cook Place.

"A lot of that is down to the landlords who don't maintain their properties, yet charge extortionate rents, and there are far too many houses, especially within London, that are left empty by their owners. Take Bakewell House as an example. There is nothing to stop the Duke renting it out to tenants and those lower down the social scale."

Now that he had got going, Eleanor plastered a rapt smile on her face and pretended to take an interest. She watched him closely, unable to shift the feeling that the man was putting on as good a performance as any given by Deanna Dacre at the Viceroy. He might espouse socialist ideals, but she doubted that he truly believed in them.

He was a fraud.

But not a fool. Certainly not that. Ann Carstairs had called him dangerous. She had better watch her step.

Peregrine, although constantly looking around, fearful that his wife might overhear him, interrupted from time to time. Eleanor considered that he made some good and well thought out arguments, but Hope-Weedon rarely answered them to her satisfaction, happy to steamroller on with the rhetoric.

She took out a cigarette which Hope-Weedon lit for her, and excused herself, saying she needed a drink and to find her friend.

What she really needed was time alone to sit and think.

She was sure, now, of many things that had previously puzzled her, though two things still eluded her. The most important of which was the whereabouts of young Joe Minshull.

"Hello, darling, glad to see you made it."

Ann appeared at her side as if from nowhere. She looked flushed and flustered.

"Oh, I've been here a while," Eleanor replied. "What happened to you? I looked everywhere for you."

"I got stuck. Just be warned that if you need to use the Studley-Gores' bathroom, that there's a dodgy lock on the door. It's taken me twenty minutes to get out and an unknown gentleman didn't bother to help. He said he couldn't wait and was going to inspect the garden."

"Oh, dear."

Eleanor couldn't help but laugh at her friend's predicament.

"It's not funny." Ann scowled.

"No, but look on the bright side. If you needed to go again, then at least you were on the inside."

Ann flicked at her fringe. "If there's a next time, you're coming with me to guard the door. Have you seen Hope-Weedon?"

"Yes, thank you. I left him boring poor old Peregrine to death."

"What a heartless woman you are. Poor Perry doesn't deserve that."

"Actually, he made more sense than Weedon. I think he was enjoying himself and winding Weedon up."

They walked to the table for more drinks.

"Well, I hope it was useful to you, anyway. What about Barbara Lancashire? Two bores in one night, eh? You're a glutton for punishment."

Eleanor buried her nose in her glass, debating how much to confide in Ann. "I know I keep asking you about that night at the Viceroy, but are you sure you didn't hear a shot?"

"Positive." Ann took the olive out of her drink and had a good swig.

"Then how come I did?"

"You were closer, that's all."

"But then, someone in the box the other side should have heard it, and everyone out the front as well."

"Maybe they did and did nothing about it. Or maybe the shot was muffled in some way. The killer may have had a silencer on the gun."

Eleanor nodded, almost to herself, and ran a thumbnail over her bottom lip. "Yes, that's a possibility. In fact...thanks, Ann. I think that's just helped solve the case."

"Oh, I have my moments." She stepped back with a laugh. "But don't offer to kiss me like the last time I helped you out, or we'll be getting entirely the wrong reputation."

"Idiot!"

"So what do we do now? Beard the killer in his den, shouting *j'accuse*, or hare round to Scotland Yard in a taxi to tell our Chief Inspector friend?"

"Neither. I'm going to go home and think it through, dotting my I's and crossing my T's. Our killer isn't going anywhere. It will wait until morning."

Chapter 25

It was barely light when Eleanor got up the next morning after a night spent trying to make sense of what she had learned at Penelope's party.

"I'll just have toast and coffee, please, Tilly, and then we must get to Bakewell House. We will need fuses and possibly flash lights and the spare key to the back door."

"Very well, my lady."

Risking indigestion in her haste, Eleanor wolfed down her breakfast and ordered the car brought around.

"It isn't far. Couldn't we walk it?" asked Tilly, as her mistress finished speaking to the man at the garage and replaced the receiver.

"I'm sorry, but I really think we should hurry."

Bakewell House stood as dark and silent as the last time Eleanor had been there. Glad that she had thought to bring the torches, she wanted still more light.

"The fuses first, Tilly. Is the box for them in the scullery?"

"Yes, my lady."

"Come on, then."

Eleanor led the way and with Tilly's assistance the fuses were put into their box. Back in the kitchen, Eleanor pressed the switch and the room flooded with light.

"That's better." She glanced around and pointed to the candles on the table. "Look, Tilly. I said there'd been someone in here, didn't I? What do you make of it?"

"Yes, you're right." The maid sniffed, but this was not her normal comment on the ways of the world. "Cigarette smoke. It's stale, but it's there, and I'll swear mother put a dust cloth over this table before she left, so that's been moved."

She strode to the window and put a hand on one of the boards. "This is loose. They must have got in this way, then put the board back."

"I wonder who it was. Is the window open?"

The maid squinted through a gap in the boards. "A fraction, possibly. Whoever did this must have jemmied it open, then pushed the board away to get in. Have you checked upstairs to see if anything's been taken?"

Eleanor shook her head. "No, but that can wait. Apart from some fine pieces of furniture which would be hard to shift, Father made sure they left nothing of value."

"Hello? What's this?"

Tilly bobbed down, disappearing from view on the far side of the table.

"What have you found?"

Eleanor put both hands on the table and leaned over, trying to see what the maid was up to.

"There's a piece of cigarette ash, and some crumbs." Tilly stood up. "Biscuit crumbs by the looks of things. Look!" She pointed towards the back door. "There's more over there. There! Do you see? Sprinkled in a line."

"As though someone were laying a trail, you mean?"

"That would be my guess."

Eleanor strode around the table, eyes on the ground. She soon saw what Tilly had seen and pulled a key out of her pocket as the maid tried the door.

"It's locked."

"Yes, and no key in it, nor hanging where it should be. Does that mean they are coming back? Never mind. Let's get it open and see where those crumbs lead."

Outside, a path ran down through the neat beds of the kitchen garden to a pair of sheds and an old lock-up garage.

Eleanor pulled the door to behind her, while Tilly bent over and inspected the path. "It's lucky it hasn't rained, I can see more crumbs up there."

"They must be leading to the garage. Come on."

"Be careful, my lady. You don't know who, or what may be in there."

No, but Eleanor knew what she hoped lay inside. The door was kept closed by a heavy wooden plank that rested on two metal brackets. Eleanor stood to one side of it.

"Wait! Perhaps I should go back for the rolling pin."

"You're as practical as ever, old girl, but I have my pistol in my pocket should I need it. Grab hold of the other end of this plank, will you. It's going to take the two of us to shift it."

They raised it up, moved it away and dropped it at the edge of the path. Then, Eleanor wrenched the door open.

"Blimey! Should I get a torch, my lady?"

Eleanor stared into the Stygian darkness and took a step inside. Something scuttled over her foot. She jumped and stepped back.

"It might be an idea at that, Tilly. Goodness knows what we'll stumble over in here without a light of some kind."

Her eyes searched the gloom, making out odd shapes, lumps, bumps, and hummocks. The tall rectangle in the far left corner might be the old grandfather clock that had stood for many years in the hall, until it had wheezed and chimed its last. A humped affair in the middle of the space might be a Chesterfield sofa or two armchairs stacked seat to seat.

Eleanor felt easier in her mind that the garage might be nothing more than a lumber room, until something rustled and slithered. She took another hasty step back. What on earth had been left in there? The garage was dry, there was no musty tang in her nostrils that would have come from damp, but she had not been living at Bakewell House when it was shut up and had no idea why the staff would have moved furniture out of drawing room, morning room or bedroom, simply to let it moulder in storage.

"Here we are, my lady. Sorry to have been so long."

Tilly switched on the torch and flashed it in a wide arc around the interior. "Merciful heavens," she cried, and nearly dropped the lamp.

Bound, blindfolded and gagged and with his arms tied behind his back, a waif-like figure lay on a broken and threadbare sofa to the right hand side of a stack of dining chairs that looked as if they might topple onto him at any minute.

"You're the nurse, Tilly. See what you can do for him. I only hope it isn't too late. I'll fetch a knife for those ropes."

"Wait, your ladyship." Tilly darted forward and touched the child's face with a gentle hand. "Praise God, he's alive. I think I can carry him into the house and we can untie him there. Can you help me lift him, please? He doesn't weigh hardly an ounce, but it's tricky with him being tied up like this."

Eleanor hurried to help, then scooped up the torch and raced ahead of Tilly back down the path to the house. She set about drawing water and putting it on to boil, then took a large kitchen knife from one of the drawers.

"Lay him on the table, Tilly. I'll find some cushions."

Between them they removed the gag, blindfold and ropes and Tilly managed to moisten his lips with water while Eleanor gently rubbed his arms, trying to help the circulation, but being extra careful not to touch his abraded wrists.

Joe suffered these ministrations with stoicism and the merest of whimpers, though he leaned into Tilly as she put an arm around his shoulder, a glass to his lips, and held him while he drank.

"Thank you," he croaked, after coughing and spluttering a good deal. Tilly patted his back.

"I don't think there's too much wrong with him, my lady, but it would be better to take him home and get a doctor to call. I can carry him to the car and wrap him in a blanket there."

"It's all right, miss. I think I can walk, but don't forget the sparklers."

"Sparklers?" queried Eleanor. "What do you mean?"

Joe pointed to the kitchen dresser. "In that drawer there."

Tilly, standing nearest, pulled it open and let out a scream. "Flaming 'eck!" She let go of the drawer as if it had burned her fingers. "Begging your pardon, my lady."

"Granted. Flaming heck, indeed."

Eleanor skirted the table and plunged both hands into the drawer. She brought up a king's ransom in emeralds, diamonds, rubies and pearls, including one necklace with a by now familiar rose-shaped clasp.

"My, my."

She swung round at a sob from behind her. Two tears rolled down Joe's grimy cheeks.

"It weren't me."

"Of course it wasn't. Come on." She crammed the jewellery into the pockets of her coat. "Let's get you home."

Despite his protests that he could walk, Tilly carried the boy to the car, while Eleanor made sure they left things at Bakewell House almost as they'd found them, and locked up.

Joe perked up at the sight of the Lagonda and pleaded to sit in the front seat.

His rescuers agreed, though Tilly still wrapped a blanket around his frail shoulders and chest before climbing into the rear.

"Please, miss, I mean my lady, will you take me home? My mum's sick an' she'll be awful worried about me."

"I will after the doctor has seen you. Your mother is getting better. I took a doctor to see her, too, and she's got some medicine. She's also got plenty of food and coal. Try and hold on a little longer, Joe, and I promise I'll take you home."

"How did you know where I live?"

Eleanor grinned at him. "I told you, I'm a detective. Remember?"

"Blimey. Guess you're a real one, after all, then."

Buoyed up by the news of his mother, and with the added excitement of being in the Lagonda, he made no mention of his aches and pains on the short trip to Bellevue Mansions.

They helped him inside, and while Eleanor telephoned for a doctor, Tilly washed his ravaged wrists and applied ointment where the ropes had chafed him. Having finished these tasks, she made him a hot drink and served him with a large slab of cake.

After the doctor had departed declaring that a bath and a good meal would be of greater use than any physic he might prescribe, and commending Tilly on the care she had already given the boy, Eleanor sent Joe off to the scullery to comply with the medic's first suggestion.

She was eager to question him and find out who had treated him so unkindly, but suppressed the desire to know more until the boy's welfare had been taken care of.

Joe, however, had every young boy's aversion to water and wasn't so sure the doctor had made the right call.

"Aw, do I 'ave to, Miss?" he complained, as the maid led him off.

"Yes. You heard him, doctor's orders. Honestly, Joe, you'll feel much better for it, and the warm water will help ease those cramped muscles of yours."

Too exhausted to argue, let alone put up a fight, he followed her meekly.

It was a different boy who stood in front of Eleanor an hour later. He still wore the same dirty and disreputable trousers, shirt, and jacket — though Tilly had done what she could with them — but now the maid's bacon and eggs followed by hot buttered toast had put a rosy glow on his cheeks and a smile on his lips. And he was clean.

"Sit down a minute, Joe. I know you are anxious to get home, but can you tell me what happened and who tied you up like that?"

Once again ignoring the chair and preferring to sit cross-legged on the floor, Joe gave a shake of his head, newly washed hair flying in all directions.

Tilly, who had come in with him, perched on the edge of the sofa, as keen to hear his story as her mistress.

"I dunno, my lady. It were dark. I'd gone round the back and seen this geezer goin' in your gate, so I followed him."

"Dear me."

"Oh, it were all right then. I kept well back and I opened the gate a bit so's I could peek through. He was just goin' in the house then, I could see that 'cause of lights in the kitchen."

As Joe launched upon his tale, it all came gushing out. How, before the door had closed and cut off the light, he had seen a party of men gathered around the kitchen table.

"I swear as they were plotting, an' I thought as they might be a bunch of thieves discussing their next job."

"Did you hear what they said?"

"Some of it, though I think some of it was foreign. One of them was definitely a toff. I could tell that by his voice, an' he kept saying 'what' at the end of everything, like what toffs do."

"I don't suppose they used any names, did they?"

"Nah, sorry, my lady, but I remember one of them asking number 3 for his report. Then he said," — Joe cleared his throat and attempted a posh voice — "seeing that number 1 is no longer with us, I suggest we stick to the plan. Vengeance can come later." He scratched his head. "Then he started talking about a game, I think, 'cause he said, 'here at 9, checkers at 11'."

Eleanor leaned forward. "Are you sure that's what he said?"

"Oh, yes. I've 'ad it running through my head ever since they tied me up and left me. I didn't want to forget it."

"Well done, this is very useful. Go on, Joe."

The boy squirmed. "There ain't much more to tell. One of the gang arrived late and caught me with my ear to the door. He threw me inside. That's when I saw the sparklers, they was lyin' on the table until the toff gathered them up and threw 'em in that drawer. There were five of them and only one of me, so there was nothing I could do to get away, honest."

"Of course not."

"Well, then they tied me up and put me in that place and the toff said they were gonna leave me there till they got back in three days time. Then they'd decide what to do with me." He looked up at Eleanor. "It's a good job you came when you did, 'cause by my reckoning that's tonight."

"Blimey!" said Tilly. "No wonder you were so hungry if you'd had nothing to eat for that long."

"Yeah, I know, and I didn't even have any biscuits after I'd laid my trail."

Eleanor made two phone calls and then they took Joe home as promised. He was allowed to sit in the front seat of the Lagonda again, an occurrence that he claimed not only made his day, but the whole terrifying ordeal worthwhile.

Mrs Minshull was delighted to see him and professed herself much improved of the flu.

"Thank you, my lady. I don't know what we would have done without your help."

"That's quite all right. Would you like to help me in return?"

Eleanor's proposition was to invite the Minshulls to move into Bakewell House.

"After all that's happened there, and Joe will tell you about that, it is obvious that I need a caretaker on the property. There is more than enough room for you and the two boys, and it is warm and dry. I will pay you three pounds a week, groceries, coal, and suitable clothing provided. What do you say?"

"But what if the gang come back, my lady?" Joe's bottom lip began to tremble.

"They won't, Joe. I'm going to get a friend of mine, and the police, and round them up tonight. Because, as God is my witness, I swear someone will pay for using my house and for what they did to you."

Chapter 26

They drove away from Cook Place and Eleanor dropped Tilly off outside Bellevue Mansions before going on to Scotland Yard. She was shown into Chief Inspector Blount's office and, refusing his offer of a chair, walked straight up to his desk.

"Good morning, my lady. What can I do for you?"

In answer, she emptied her pockets and laid her booty before him. "You can return all this to its rightful owners, please."

"Stap me!"

It was the second time in their acquaintance that she had left him speechless and she laughed at his stunned face before finally sitting in the chair opposite.

"Where the blue blazes —" he began, when he recovered the power of speech.

"In my own home."

"Uh huh. In your own home?"

"Yes, in a drawer in the kitchen dresser, but I didn't steal them."

"Really? And I suppose you're going to tell me next who killed Sir David Bristol?"

"Yes." She flashed him a pretty smile and told him the whole story.

While she talked, the fire in the room crackled in the grate and Blount doodled on his pad, making cats and kittens out of circles and curves. From time to time he sat back and inspected his handiwork before starting another. He didn't interrupt, though neither did he miss a word, and once murmured, "so, that was it. I did wonder," as if Eleanor had solved a puzzle for him.

"I've been in touch with Major Armitage from Military Intelligence," she said in conclusion, "because the jewels were stolen to fund the activities of a spy ring that he thinks was headed up by Sir David. I am to ask if you could have a party of men in Berkeley Square later tonight. He will contact you later to make arrangements."

"Him again, eh? I might have known he'd be involved. Very well, I'll speak to the major as and when."

"And, I'd like to ask you a favour."

She started to separate the string of pearls from the jumble of necklaces and bracelets on the desk.

"You want to keep that one, do you?"

"Certainly not! I — oh!" Eleanor looked up to see Chief Inspector Blount grinning at her and realised she was being teased by the avuncular policeman.

"These are what started it all off." She picked up the pearls and ran them through her hands, appreciating the soft opalescent sheen of them and the glittering ice of the diamond clasp. "These are why I became involved. I was given the job of finding the necklace, you see, and now that I have, I'd like to return the pearls to Lady Lancashire."

"They are hers, I take it?"

"Oh, yes, undoubtedly."

Blount nodded. "Yes, all right. I don't see why not. I'll get the rest of these gewgaws put away in the safe and call my sergeant."

"You may need to take a constable as well. There is something you need to ask or search for."

She gave him the details and watched his eyes widen.

"Well, we'll ask. I can always get a search warrant if necessary. Are you in your own car?"

"Yes, I am."

"Good, then we'll follow you to Eaton Place."

Barbara Lancashire was delighted to see her pearls again, but not so pleased to see Eleanor nor her accompanying police escort.

"Really, Lady Eleanor! What is all this?" she exclaimed when Chief Inspector Blount and Sergeant Hale had been introduced.

"Is your husband at home, my lady?" asked Blount.

"Yes. What do you want with him? He's a very busy man."

But even a man of Sir Robert's standing couldn't be too busy to see the police, Eleanor thought. She hadn't missed the flash of fear in Barbara's eyes, and wondered if she knew, or even suspected the truth.

"We'll explain all that when he joins us, if you don't mind," said Blount. "Will you call him, please?"

"Oh, very well."

She rang for a footman then, with an ill grace, invited them to sit down. Eleanor sank into an easy chair, the sergeant perched on the edge of a sofa, but Blount remained standing, looking stolid and earnest in the middle of the hearth rug.

"Where did you find my necklace, Lady Eleanor?" Barbara asked as they waited for her husband. She put the pearls into a drawer in the walnut bureau.

"In a very unlikely place, as it happens."

"I trust the thief has been apprehended."

Eleanor gave nothing away. "The main thing is, they are back in your possession." About to add that all's well that ends well, she stopped herself in the nick of time. It was all about to end very badly indeed for Barbara Lancashire.

"You wanted me, my dear?"

The door opened to admit a grey-haired man in his late fifties. Short and round, with a pair of thick-lensed glasses on the end of his thin nose, Lord Lancashire was not a prepossessing figure. He shuffled in a pair of carpet slippers to his wife's chair and put a hand on her shoulder.

"I wasn't told we had visitors."

She smiled tremulously up at him. "Yes, Robert. I'm sure you know the Duke of Bakewell's daughter, Lady Eleanor, and these gentlemen are from Scotland Yard."

"Yes, my lord. I'm Chief Inspector Blount and this is Sergeant Hale. I understand you and your wife were at the Viceroy theatre last week on the evening Sir David Bristol was murdered."

"Yes, yes, that is so. I gave our names to the constable at the time." He looked down at his wife. "That's right, isn't it, dear?"

"Yes, Robert, you did, and I told him that we had seen and heard nothing of murder. Our eyes had been on the stage watching Miss Dacre's thrilling performance. I said the same to you, Lady Eleanor, if you remember. When you called on me yesterday, I mean."

"Did you leave your box at any time, my lord? During the second act?"

"No, I don't think so, Chief Inspector. As my wife says, Miss Dacre was on stage and I...I didn't want to miss anything."

Blount scowled at his lordship. "Yet Lady Eleanor here says that you were missing from your box towards the end of the act."

"Lady Eleanor is wrong," Barbara snapped. She glared at Eleanor through eyes reduced to slits. "Sir Robert was with me the whole time."

"I suppose I may have gone to the bathroom, yes, I think possibly I did." Lancashire smiled, pleased with an excuse that, after his wife's claim, came too late.

Barbara had seen the danger, however and took steps to avert it.

"Really, Chief Inspector, I'm sure that Lady Eleanor means well, but I shouldn't take her word over ours. Now that she has set herself up as a detective, even if she is genteel enough to call it an enquiry agent, she clearly thinks she has something to prove. A lot of young gels are getting themselves jobs these days, but that doesn't mean they have the expertise to do them and I fear that Lady Eleanor is a case in point. She is simply mistaken in this instance."

She bestowed a condescending smile, first on Blount, then on Eleanor. The latter said nothing. She had nothing to prove to the Chief Inspector. He knew her track record, short though it was.

What's more, Barbara's prattling interference had brought attention back on herself.

"How long had Sir David been blackmailing you to pass on state secrets, my lady?" Blount demanded.

"Oh!" Barbara went white and put her head in her hands.

"I take it you were aware of this, Sir Robert? Is that why you shot him?"

"Nonsense, man!"

"But you knew —"

Sir Robert pulled himself upwards to his full height. It didn't help. He was, Eleanor thought, too short to be imposing.

"My wife told me yesterday that the bounder was blackmailing her over gambling debts. He threatened to expose her in that scurrilous rag of his if she didn't hand over a particularly fine pearl necklace of hers. Barbara has no access to state secrets. Preposterous to say otherwise."

Eleanor surveyed the Lancashires. After her visit yesterday, Barbara must have concocted that story for her husband's benefit and to cover her sins. Eleanor wondered if he had already known, and if Barbara had suspected him of solving her problems. Or did she, even now, think that an unknown killer had been her benefactor?

And what of Robert? Was he truly in the dark about the nature of the blackmail?

It would be up to Chief Inspector Blount to decide if there was a case to be made against either of them. Eleanor remained silent as she listened to his interrogation.

"Were you aware, sir, that the necklace in question had been stolen, until Lady Eleanor here returned it to your wife on our arrival?"

"I knew of its theft, though not of its return. That is good news." He beamed at Eleanor before turning to his wife. "I'm glad you have your pearls back."

"But you weren't aware that your wife was using those pearls to pass messages to Sir David Bristol?"

Sir Robert's brow furrowed. "I'm sorry, Chief Inspector, I am at a loss to know how she would do that?"

"By letting him know, simply by virtue of which shoulder the clasp was positioned on, which of two days Mr Gaston Doumergue would be at Chequers."

"What?" Sir Robert gripped the back of his wife's chair, the blood draining from his florid cheeks.

"Did you leave that information lying about on your desk, Sir Robert? Does her ladyship have access to your safe?"

Lord Lancashire appeared not to hear the questions as he stared at his wife. "I...I...Barbara? Is this true?"

She said nothing, though the twisting, writhing fingers in her lap seemed to semaphore her guilt.

"Answer me, woman? Is this true?"

The fingers fluttered and flew. "A mere taradiddle."

Apparently satisfied, Sir Robert faced the policeman. "There, you see. Besides, why on earth would Bristol need to know about the Frenchman's whereabouts?"

"Because he was the leader of a coven of spies who planned to assassinate him."

"Good heavens! Surely not. Bristol? I can scarcely believe it."

"Nevertheless, we have evidence to that effect."

"But why?"

Blount was saved from answering Sir Robert by a tap on the door and the arrival of his constable. Over his arm he carried the jacket of a man's evening suit.

Eleanor glanced at Barbara who was eyeing both jacket and constable with horror.

"Found it, sir. It had been put out for collection by the rag man."

"Good man. And?"

"You were right, sir. There's a bullet hole in it. Possibly some powder marks, too."

"Let's have a look." Blount stretched out a hand.

"And the staff assure me this was the suit that Sir Robert wore on the night he and her ladyship went to the theatre, sir."

He sounded rather pleased with himself. Eleanor hid a smile, delighted that they had found the evidence she had told Blount to look for.

The Chief Inspector turned the garment in his hands and opened it up, holding it by the shoulders. It had several holes where it had been folded over, wrapped around the gun, and used to muffle the sound of the shot. The single bullet had torn through all the layers on its way to the man in box number 11.

The Lancashires had no answer to Blount's questions as to how the jacket had got into that state. The pair appeared to shrink into themselves, all the bluster and pomposity drained out of them, leaving only shrivelled husks, as they stared at the evidence of their guilt. Blount arrested them, and as the sergeant and constable led them away, turned to Eleanor.

"It isn't over, you realise, but I think we have a better chance of getting the truth out of them now." He bowed and raised her hand to his lips. "Thank you, your ladyship."

Eleanor inclined her head, but said nothing. The Chief Inspector was right, it wasn't over. Barbara may have betrayed her husband, and Sir Robert committed murder, but they still had a nest of spies to lay by the heels and bring to justice.

And there was the small matter of a young boy to be avenged.

Chapter 27

Promptly at eight o'clock that evening, Eleanor and Tilly slipped inside Bakewell House and made their quiet way by torchlight to the kitchen. Under strict instructions from Major Armitage to stay out of sight and out of trouble, the pair stepped into the scullery and held a whispered conversation.

"Should we take the fuses out again?" Tilly shivered in the cold night air.

"I don't think there's any point. The gang will assume there's no light on like before, so they won't try the switch."

"But what if they do?"

Knowing that she was in her own home on sufferance did not please Eleanor. Armitage had been confident, once Eleanor had told him of the gang's plans and how many people were involved, to handle everything himself with assistance from Chief Inspector Blount if need be. He had been less than sanguine, however, about her own and Tilly's presence. Only when she had suggested that he think of them as back-up did he accede to her request to take part in the night's events.

"Then I suppose that will be the signal to the Major and his team to swoop in and grab them. They won't do that though until all five of the members have arrived. Are you armed?"

"In a manner of speaking."

Both women were good shots, and Eleanor had her own small pistol tucked into the pocket of her trousers. They both wore black from head to foot.

"I hope you don't have to use it. The gang are probably all armed. If they start shooting, go to the floor and keep your head down. I'm going to stand on the other side of the service door. Will you be all right here?"

"Yes, I'll stay here in the scullery, but keep the door ajar, so I can hear what's going off."

"All right. Good luck."

The two shared a quick embrace and separated. Eleanor walked back through the kitchen and the swing door to take up a position in the hallway beyond. She leant against the side of the grand staircase and shivered in the silent darkness — a shiver that owed as much to the familiar thrill of danger and excitement as it did to the cold.

Between them, she and Tilly had both entrances covered. The maid was only a step from the back door and would be safe enough if she stayed inside the scullery. No one was likely to come in via the front door, but if they did, or if they came out of the kitchen, Eleanor would see them.

She fondled the pistol in her pocket and waited for the man who had savagely bound up a young boy and left him to die, alone and frightened, in an unused garage. Given the chance she would shoot him herself.

The wait seemed endless until, suddenly, the night erupted into noise. Eleanor heard shouts and shots. An urge to leave her safe position overwhelmed her. What if Tilly, or worse, the Major were hurt? What if her quarry got away?

She took a deep breath to steady herself and then stepped closer to the service door, straining her ears for sounds from the kitchen. To her dismay she heard the waspish tones she'd hoped never to hear again.

"You fool! You've brought us into a trap."

"How was I to know the place was under surveillance? They've got the others, I think. It's just us, now."

"Maybe we can get out through the front."

"Nah, it's bound to be watched, what? Besides, the door will be locked and I don't have that key. First, I'll get the jewels, then we may have to shoot it out."

"I'm unarmed."

That was enough for Eleanor. She hadn't cared for the odds with two guns against her, but one she could handle.

She stepped through the door.

Gerald Hope-Weedon was standing by the dresser, a gun in one hand, a flash light in the other, staring open-mouthed into the empty drawer. Behind him, just to the side of the open back door, Miss Haringay looked on.

Despite the torch in Weedon's hand, Eleanor's silent entry had gone unnoticed.

"All right, Gerald. Put the gun down and your hands up, please." He spun to face her, gun raised.

Eleanor's pistol pointed straight at him and, as he turned, Eleanor caught sight of Peter Armitage in the doorway. With a cat-like stealth the major took a step forward. He placed one arm around the secretary's neck with the hand over her mouth, while at the same time wrapping his other arm around her waist. Then he lifted her up and whisked her out of the kitchen. It was a slick, well-practised, and above all silent manoeuvre and Hope-Weedon had heard nothing, his attention being focussed first on the empty drawer, and then on Eleanor.

"Put the gun down," she said, again. "I do know how to use this little bauble in my hand. I'm a crack shot and my aim is deadly. Besides, at this range, I can't miss."

Neither could he. In her anger, she ignored that fact.

He shook his head. "I could shoot you dead, and plead self-defence."

"Not when you're a trespasser in my house. I ought to kill you where you stand for what you did to that boy. How dare you? And how dare you use my home for your filthy purpose, you two-faced coward?"

Her finger tightened on the trigger.

"Ella! No!"

The major, having somehow rid himself of his burden, had returned to the open doorway. At his command, Eleanor wavered, instincts torn.

For a moment, the three of them stood there like statues, guns raised in the semi-dark, before light flooded the kitchen and the scullery door burst open. Tilly flew out and, with a scream of agony, Hope-Weedon went down, clutching his knee.

His gun lay on the floor. Eleanor stepped forward and retrieved it as the room filled with men. They dragged the politician to his feet and took him away, hobbling badly, muttering imprecations, claiming his kneecap was broken.

Tilly leant back against the dresser and watched them go, her arms crossed on her chest, her rolling pin sticking up like a truncheon.

Armitage ran a hand over his lower face, hiding a grin.

"Wait there, please, ladies. I shan't be long."

When he returned, he did so with Chief Inspector Blount, who came in rubbing his hands. Eleanor and Tilly were seated at the table.

"A good night's work, I'd say, Major."

"Did you get them all?" Eleanor asked, motioning them to chairs.

"Yes," Blount said, lowering his large frame onto a seat. "All five of them. Four men, one woman."

"Who bites." Armitage wrapped a handkerchief around his hand.

"But I thought Joe said five men?" Tilly looked at her mistress.

"He was mistaken. Miss Haringay probably had her back to him, or was hidden in the shadows. Did she draw blood?" She pointed at Armitage's makeshift bandage.

"No, it's only bruised."

"Well, together with the arrest of Sir Robert Lancashire, it's been a good day's work all round." Blount beamed at the two women. "Thank you, my lady, Miss Tilly."

"You're welcome." Eleanor inclined her head, then looked at Armitage. "And your French visitor...?"

"Has been safely ensconced at Chequers for the last few hours. I've a man keeping an eye on things there, together with a few policemen from the local force."

"Good. By the bye, Chief Inspector, Gerald Hope-Weedon is your jewel thief. I've managed to discover that he had been invited to quite a few of the parties and soirées where the jewels were taken. You would need to check if he attended any others, but I'm sure you'll find that he did."

"Right you are."

"I had originally assumed that the jewels had been stolen to fund the gang's activities, but finding them all here, I'm beginning to think they may have been taken merely to line his own pockets."

"And it was Sir David who was in charge of the gang?"

"Yes, that's right." Eleanor smiled at her maid, still cradling the rolling pin. She'd told Joe Minshull that she had more than one use for it, Eleanor recalled. It was true, as Gerald Hope-Weedon could testify.

"But why?"

It was the same question that Robert Lancashire had asked only an hour or two earlier.

"Money, Tilly. As Major Armitage will tell you, as well as being a newspaper proprietor, Sir David sold armaments. I saw a map when I was in Miss Haringay's office. Along with quite a few European capital cities, there were several Middle Eastern and African states marked on it, and in small letters at the bottom it bore the label, 'Arms Sales'. If he could foment another war, it would increase his profits."

Tilly sniffed. "That's disgusting."

"As for Hope-Weedon, his reasons were more idealogical, but even so, he is a hypocrite. He aims to be the top man at everything and I rather think that he and Bristol were at loggerheads."

"He wanted to run the gang?"

All the time that Eleanor had been talking, she'd been acutely aware of Peter Armitage sitting opposite, saying nothing, a small private smile on his lips. She looked directly at him and nodded.

"Oh, yes, just as he wants to be Foreign Secretary, and possibly Prime Minister. As it happens, Sir Robert Lancashire is notoriously forgetful. Ask anyone who knows him. It's my guess that the itinerary for Ramsay MacDonald's guest this evening was left lying about on Sir Robert's desk or in an unlocked drawer, and that Hope-Weedon discovered it on the night of Barbara's soirée. Bristol was killed, you see, before he could pass on Barbara's information, yet the gang still knew which night they had to be at Chequers."

Later, Eleanor stood at the back door while Peter Armitage pressed her hand to his lips. She had already said goodnight to Chief Inspector Blount, who was ambling down the kitchen garden towards the back gate.

"Well done, my lady, and thank you."

"I'm glad to have been of assistance." She smiled. He hung onto her hand.

"Are you going to continue as a private enquiry agent?"

"Why not? I seem to be rather good at it."

She had effectively solved three cases and Peter Armitage was holding her hand for an awfully long time.

"Then, I'm sure I will see you again soon."

Eleanor heard the expected sniff and reluctantly retrieved her hand. Tomorrow she would visit Deanna Dacre and give Danny Danvers his scoop. For tonight, though, her eyes sparkled with laughter and all was right with the world.

The End

THANK YOU FOR READING *A Burglary In Belgravia.* I hope you enjoyed it.

Book 1 of Eleanor and Tilly's adventures, is *A Poisoning in Piccadilly.*

Book 3, *A Traitor At Tower Bridge* is available for pre-order. You can reserve your copy here:

https://www.amazon.com/dp/B07ZD2DFM5

https://www.amazon.co[1].uk[2]/dp/B07ZD2DFM5[3]

Other series by Lynda Wilcox:

The Verity Long Mysteries[4]

A crime writer's researcher finds herself in a heap of trouble trying to solve old cases.

The Gemini Detectives[5]

Twins Linzi and Loren Repton solve crimes with the help of a mysterious bag-lady and her three-legged dog.

Be the first to know of new books at low prices, sales, free offers, and more! Sign up for my New Release mailing list: http://eepurl.com/r0jRf

---

1.   https://www.amazon.com/dp/B07ZD2DFM5

2.   https://www.amazon.com/dp/B07ZD2DFM5

3.   https://www.amazon.com/dp/B07ZD2DFM5

4.   https://www.amazon.com/gp/product/B07FK8S5WK?ref_=series_rw_dp_labf

5.   https://www.amazon.com/gp/product/B07DP8ZBX5?ref_=series_rw_dp_labf

Made in the USA
Middletown, DE
15 December 2020